FIC BUR

Burton, Hester.
The flood at Reedsmere.

FIL
Bur

Mark and Mary Vaughn and an American
friend set out in a rubber dinghy to rescue
their neighbors, trapped by flood waters
sweeping over the English coast.

THE FLOOD AT REEDSMERE

Books by Hester Burton

THE FLOOD AT REEDSMERE

NO BEAT OF DRUM

TIME OF TRIAL

CASTORS AWAY!

The
Flood at
Reedsmere

HESTER BURTON

Illustrated by Robin Jacques

THE WORLD PUBLISHING COMPANY

CLEVELAND AND NEW YORK

Published by The World Publishing Company
2231 West 110th Street, Cleveland, Ohio 44102
First American Edition 1968
Library of Congress catalog card number: 68–15273
Text copyright © Hester Burton
Illustrations copyright © Robin Jacques
Designed by Jack Jaget

To Catharine

Contents

Contents

ACKNOWLEDGMENTS

I am indebted to the British Broadcasting Corporation for allowing me to use the texts of their News Summaries at the time of the great gale, and to the *Eastern Daily Press* for giving me access to past issues of their newspapers.

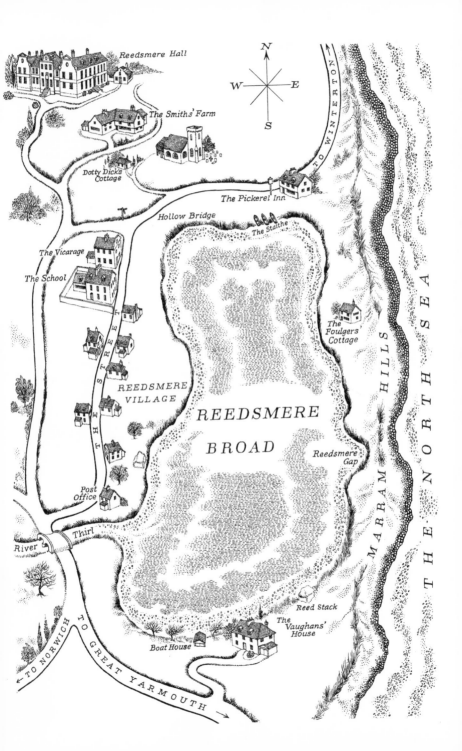

THE FLOOD AT REEDSMERE

Reedsmere

This is the story of what happened to a village in Norfolk one winter night, early in 1953. It is the story of everyone who lived in that village.

It is the story of Canon Crowfoot, the vicar of Reedsmere, and of Dan Ball, the village drunkard; of Sir Bartlett and Lady Speke up at the Hall and of Jim Foulger, the fishmonger, who for the past forty years had been poaching Sir Bartlett's game. If you have a moment to waste in the Pickerel Inn, Ben Blaza will still tell you what he did that January night when he hurriedly locked his till and climbed out of the window of the bar. And old Mr. Clatworthy, who is ninety now, still starts in his sleep, dreaming that he is back in it all again.

Yet it is to the boys and girls of Reedsmere, rather than to the grownups, that the story really belongs.

The grownups had lived through wars and air raids and all manner of frightening misfortunes, but that Saturday night was the first extraordinary thing that had ever happened to their sons and daughters. It was a landmark, a turning point in their lives.

Oddly enough, it was not in the howling wind of Saturday that the story began, but two days earlier—in the middle of Thursday morning, a morning so quiet and sunny and beautiful that the voices of the boys and girls in the school playground rang out clear and sharp as they do on a summer's

13

day. The reed cutters could hear them nearly a mile away, as they stacked the reeds down on the edge of the Broad. Canon Crowfoot smiled at them as he sat in his garden, wrapped up in coats and rugs, writing his Candlemas sermon.

"What a day!" exclaimed Dr. Vaughan, as he slung his black maternity case into the back of his car. "What a beautiful day!"

It all began with a cow.

"Bet yer've never ridden a cow," taunted Ned Brewster.

"Bet you I can," replied Mark Vaughan.

The two boys were leaning moodily over one of Farmer Catchpole's gates, far down on the marsh, near the Reedsmere Gap.

"Bet yer can't ride that one," jeered Ned, pointing to a large-bellied Friesian, quietly browsing the grass on the edge of a dike.

"Bet I will," said Mark, unlatching the gate and running into the field.

Quite suddenly it was of the greatest importance to him that he, Mark, should vault on to that broad cow's back and ride triumphantly up and down the dike in front of a confounded and admiring Ned.

"Gar'n," shouted Ned from the gate, "she'll toss yer in the water."

"Gar'n to you," yelled back Mark.

He could not afford the flourish of a running jump. The ground was too spongy and uneven, and the cow too big. Instead, he clambered up the cow's side and straddled her somewhere in the middle.

"There you are!" grinned Mark. He could not take time off to look at Ned, because at any moment he expected the cow to throw up her back legs or to rear up her head. But the cow took no notice of him. She went on quietly munching her tuft of grass.

"Yew've got to ride her now," yelled Ned.

It was like trying to ride a sofa. The stretch was so wide that it pulled at the muscles in his thighs.

"Yew've got to make her go," repeated Ned.

Mark slid himself back on to the cow's narrower, bony rump and gently pressed his knees into her flanks.

"Come on, cow," he said encouragingly. "Come on, cow, walk about a bit."

But not a foot would the cow move. She merely raised her head and looked back at him reprovingly, slobbering a little as she did so.

Suddenly Ned roared with laughter. It was a friendly, joyous kind of laugh.

"Yew don't 'arf look a fool," he shouted, "sittin' there doin' nothin' on the back of that silly old cow."

The sound of his voice rippled out over the sunny winter marsh and out over the glinting little waves on Reedsmere Broad. For Mark, perched up high on the rump of the cow, the whole morning suddenly broke into a smile. He let go his knee grip and allowed himself to fall off backward over the cow's tail.

"Thank goodness," he thought as he sat in the sopping marsh. "We're not going to quarrel after all."

The boys had finished with the cow. They ran off down the reed cutter's lane toward the Vaughans' house and never thought of her again. But the cow, a little put out perhaps by their rude interruptions of her morning thoughts, slowly reared her head from the grass, slowly lumbered toward the open gate, and slowly plodded east toward the sea. With the blundering innocence of all her kind, she decided to do something she had never done before in her life.

Feeling the sun warm on her flanks and smelling the tang in the salt air, she frisked up her tail and almost galloped along the landward slope of the Marram Hills. After the soggy mud of her marsh, the soft, dry sand felt pleasant to her feet, and the coarse tussocks of marram grass gave a rough, friendly brush against her legs.

When she came to Reedsmere Gap she stood with her two front feet on the low, rotting, sandbag wall and gazed out at the gray North Sea. She did nothing else to begin this story. She just stood there mooing gently, staring at the slow unending march of the waves and pawing a little with her sharp cloven feet.

As she pawed, first one rotting sandbag split, and then another, and then another. And the sand slowly drained out of that pitiable, forgotten sea defense and got blown by the breeze into little ribbed drifts along the pebbly beach.

And the cow went on standing there mooing softly to herself, contemplating the sea.

Back in the village school it was nearly time for morning recess.

Outside, on top of Canon Crowfoot's garden wall, with her feet dangling over on the side of the school playground, nervously plucking at the rank-smelling ivy, sat a girl of thirteen.

Mary Vaughan looked cold and forlorn.

Two years ago, the playground had been her playground as well as Myrtle's and Sally's and Jenny's. She gazed sadly at the great chestnut tree in the corner, where the conkers came spluttering down so richly in every September wind; and she stared at the netball post and the worn place in the grass where she and Myrtle had always skipped. She wondered, for a moment, whether Latin and chemistry at the Emily Davies High School really made up for the fun that she and all the others used to have down there.

The school bell rang.

Out into the playground jostled the boys and girls of Reedsmere School, jumping up and down, pushing and shouting—running to get out into the winter sun. Mary picked out Myrtle Beamish straightway, for her carroty head of hair bobbed about among the other girls like a brave, gay flag. There she was by the netball post; and now, having seen Mary sitting on the wall, she came and stood on the grass below.

"Hullo," said Myrtle.

"Hullo," replied Mary.

"Come down and play."

Mary shook her head.

Myrtle's stare slowly turned hostile. Deep down in her stolid Norfolk heart someone whispered, "She's stuck up, is Mary Vaughan; the likes o' you 'en't good enough for her any more."

"Why not?" asked Myrtle crossly.

"I'm measly."

Myrtle took the hair out of her eyes and had another look at Mary. Now she came.to think of it, Mary didn't look at all stuck up; she just looked cold and white and miserable.

"Measly? When d'yew git it?"

"A fortnight ago. I'm not out of quarantine till Saturday."

"Nuts!" exclaimed Myrtle energetically. "Come on down. I've had the measles lots of times."

Mary slipped off the wall and stood in the playground in front of her friend. She looked surprisingly long and thin.

"Cor, yer posh!" exclaimed Myrtle, examining the cut of Mary's long blue jeans.

"I think it's you that's posh," said Mary.

In her flared green corduroy skirt and royal blue jumper Myrtle looked bright and capable and definite, as though she were announcing an inescapable truth to the world.

"Hev an enniseed ball."

Mary hated aniseed balls, but it was so kind of Myrtle to be offering her one that she smiled and took it and put it in the side of her cheek, shutting it out from the rest of her mouth behind her clenched back teeth.

"We've git a new skipping rhyme since yew were here," volunteered Myrtle. "Ever so silly. Like to hear it?"

Two girls were turning a rope and two other girls were skipping over it a few yards away, and as they skipped they sang:

> "A monkey came to my shop
> I asked him what he wanted
> A loaf, sir. A loaf, sir.
> Where's yer money?
> In me pocket
> Where's yer pocket?
> I en't got it
> Well out yew bunk."

"Silly, en't it?"

"Very," laughed Mary.

The two girls made room for the newcomers, and when Myrtle and Mary had skipped the rhyme, they ran off warm and happy, and walked round and round the playground with their arms linked behind each other's back. It was a thing one did in Reedsmere with one's best friend.

Suddenly Myrtle began to giggle.

"Oh, Mary, that enniseed ball," she laughed.

Mary smiled.

"I know it must look awfully funny sticking out of my cheek."

"No, it en't that," said Myrtle. "I've just remembered yew hate enniseed balls. Spit it out, quick."

Mary was just about to do so, when Myrtle clapped her hand over her mouth.

"Yew've forgotten," she exclaimed.

So Mary had.

Solemnly the two girls walked toward Canon Crowfoot's garden wall. They stood in a special place—where the wisteria hung over from the other side.

"Now," said Myrtle.

Mary blew with all her might. The aniseed ball shot up into the air and over the wall. On the other side, it fell with a clatter on the corrugated tin roof of the vicar's potting shed.

"Oh, Mary," sighed Myrtle. "Yer just as good as ever yew were!"

In the Vaughans' playroom, things were not going nearly so well.

Since it was at Mark's invitation that Ned had played truant from school, it was more than usually important that the morning should be a success. The two boys had nearly quarreled by Farmer Catchpole's gate and now, in the playroom, another storm was brewing.

Mark had smuggled Ned home to show him his treasures. He had begun with the orchids he had found last summer in the Cotswolds and which he had pressed carefully between sheets of pink blotting paper. But Ned had said that the orchids were dull old things and ought to be thrown in the fire. Then he had shown him his grandfather's collection of moths. This had amused his guest rather better, and Ned had gone back twice to look at the one with the skull marks on its head. But there is an end, even to moths.

Now, Mark was showing him the bits of pottery that he had picked up yesterday in the field at Caister.

"That's a bit of Samian wine bottle," he announced.

"Gar'n," said Ned. "Looks like one of me dad's broken flower pots."

Mark flushed with anger. He wanted to bash Ned's freckled nose against his silly freckled face. But he was terribly hampered. He was the host.

Looking around urgently for some way of saving the morning, his eye fell on his catapult.

"Like to go out and pot at things?" he suggested desperately.

"Don't mind if I do," grinned Ned.

First they potted at Mrs. Vaughan's dish towels hanging up to dry and then at the ugly granite balls on the top of the gate post. Then they wandered off along the upper road above the village, and then downhill in the direction of the church.

The men were carting manure in the fifty-acre field behind the churchyard; the boys could hear them talking to each other as they walked along Hollow Bottom Lane. They could smell the sweet smell of the horse dung and see the thin wisps of steam rising from the hundred little heaps of muck.

"Better keep low under the hedge," muttered Ned to Mark. "Don't want me Uncle Nick to see I'm not in school."

Except for the holiday mood of the sun, what an ordinary work-a-day morning it was!

Tom Mobbs, the verger, polished the brasses on the Speke family tomb. Up at the Hall, Sir Bartlett cleaned his guns. Down in his cottage in Reedsmere Street, old Mr. Clatworthy stole his wife's best dustpan and brush and swept out the floor of the canary cage. From every kitchen in the village came the clatter of saucepans and the beginning of the dinner smell. Five seagulls swooped on to the Canon's newly dug potato patch and squawked so loud that the vicar woke up with a start.

Mrs. Vaughan was ordering the week's groceries from Mrs. Beamish in the post office and general store.

"So glad the children are better," smiled Mrs. Beamish. "It's a worriting thing the measles. I never did like them, not even when our Myrtle caught them—and she's as strong as a horse."

"It wasn't a bad attack," said Mrs. Vaughan. "And they're both off to school on Monday. So if you could send the ladyfingers and the confectioners' sugar and the cream on Saturday . . ."

"A treat for them before they go back, I'll be bound," said Mrs. Beamish, smiling. "I'll send Myrtle."

In the Pickerel Inn, Dan Ball sat over his second pint of beer and stared wearily out of the window at the reeds and the Broad and the roofs of the village beyond.

"What a dump of a place!" he sighed. "What a dump! Nothin's happened in Reedsmere, not in a thousand years."

And down on the shore, at the Gap, the grains of sand trickled out of the sandbags that the cow had torn—one by one, relentlessly, like the sand running out in an hourglass.

The Vaughans

On Friday the fog returned.

For eighteen days that January it had hung over the Norfolk coast like an evil dream—muffling the eyes and ears and driving people's thoughts inward upon themselves. Day after day the ships in Yarmouth Roads had wailed plaintively with their sirens, warning one another that they were out there alone, moving eyeless and lost in the thick blanket of fog.

After breakfast Mark ran down to the boathouse with the pieces of toast that no one had eaten. He stood on the edge of the quay, straining his ears for the chuckle of a moorhen and his eyes for the sight of a grebe or a coot. But the Broad seemed dead. Not a sound came to him through the weaving mist, and not a single bird bobbed up at his feet. He let the toast drop into the water and watched it float soggily away. Then he turned toward the house, kicking at the gravel as he went. The fog made him feel frustrated and bored and cross.

None of them felt their best.

Up in Mark's bedroom, while making his bed, Mrs. Vaughan found a squashed snail shell under the pillow. At the beginning of the holidays she would have been amused. Today she was exasperated.

"He's an impossible boy!" she exclaimed to herself. "He's untidy and thoughtless and completely idiotic. Whoever heard of a boy going to bed with a snail under his pillow?"

She looked around his room, nerving herself to note the mess that it was in.

On the rug by his bed lay a tie and a shoe. His new Rugby ball sat perched in the round of the lamp. A sponge bag full of flints had spilled out under the chest of drawers, and flung down near the window lay several pieces of screwed-up paper, a copy of *Kidnapped,* and dozens of shriveled nuts. Over all, in the slight draft that blew from under the door, scurried the remains of a packet of foreign stamps.

"And I tidied it only yesterday," she sighed wearily, as she folded down the sheet.

"Drat the boy," gasped his father, as he tumbled over Mark's Rugby boots, thrown down on the front doorstep.

Those two long days, before it all began, were indelibly imprinted upon Mary's mind. It was not that they were exciting or even pleasant days to remember; it was just that they were the last days, the very last days, that she and Mark were ever quite like that again.

"Yes," she would think afterward, "we were just like that. That was Mark, kicking round the house, pent-up and bored and longing to explode. And that was me, sitting at the piano, turning over the Bach preludes and not being able to choose which one to play."

She supposed it was the fog that made them all so blind.

It was not a time to fuss about untidy rooms. Not a time for self-reproach. Not a time for anger. Not even for justice.

Yet the sword of justice fell with a clang in the middle of Saturday lunch.

Dr. Vaughan had come in late.

"Well?" he asked, sitting down and looking at Mark.

"Well what, Dad?"

"Have you got anything to tell me?"

"What sort of thing?"

"Have you done something in the last few days that you should not have done?"

Mark went through Thursday and Friday rapidly in his mind. Was it the cow? But the cow hadn't minded him riding on her back. It couldn't be the cow.

He shook his head.

"Nothing very awful, Dad, honestly."

Then the dreadful thing happened. Their father—their gentle, kind, rather absent-minded father—suddenly exploded in anger.

"I can forgive you for being naughty and high-spirited, Mark, but I can never forgive you for being a coward."

"A coward!" exclaimed Mark, horror-struck.

"You've broken an old man's window, and you haven't got the courage to own up."

"What old man? Where?"

"Old Richard Dack. He lives down the lane past the church."

A gleam of understanding crossed Mark's face. The catapult. Ned Brewster. Thursday morning. How could he have forgotten that sound of breaking glass?

"Do you mean that dreadful tumbledown little place all covered with ivy? I didn't know Dotty Dick lived there. Oh, Dad, I really didn't. I thought it was condemned and empty, I really did. It's got ivy growing all over the windows."

"You knew you had broken some glass?"

"Yes."

"When you break someone else's glass you have to pay for it. Why didn't you tell me about it before?"

"I thought it just wasn't important, Dad," said Mark with tears gathering under his lashes. "It looked such a horrible place. There's shepherd's purse and dead nettles growing out of the ·thatch. I couldn't believe anyone was living there. I just didn't think."

"Well, it's time you were taught to think."

What an unspeakable thing to have happened. Father angry, and Mark to be punished as a coward!

Mary fled from the room and ran out through the garden and across the marsh, holding her hands over her ears, like the picture of Christian fleeing from the City of Destruction.

"I can never forgive you for being a coward," rang in the wind and the grass and the reeds. "I can never forgive you for being a coward."

"And poor Mark is silly and thoughtless," sobbed Mary. "But he's as brave as a bull."

The rising wind had blown away the fog. Mary struggled straight into the wind, the legs of her jeans flapping harshly like wet flags and her brown hair tossing upward and back in its gusts. Every now and then she stumbled over a tuft of marram grass and sent a spume of sand puffing down the coast. Below her on her right, the North Sea heaved and fell in a dark sullen swell; below her on her left a great sweep of Norfolk stretched flat and wide to the trees behind the Hall. Stumbling along the top of the sandy ridge of dunes, she felt as though she were walking on the rim of the world.

The clouds were sweeping down the coast, some ragged and curled, others massed in great battalions, like a huge army moving into battle. She looked up to watch them overhead, and tripped over a tuft of grass.

The jolt upset her.

"It's no good. It's no good," she sobbed deep down inside herself, as she knelt in the sand. Not even the roaring east coast wind, that almost blew the breath out of one's body and the wits out of one's brain, would blow this misery away.

She crawled through the coarse grass and the sand and the dead lupin stems till she dropped out of the wind on the seaward side of the ridge. Then she sat down, determined to face all that there was to face.

Her father, whom she loved, had been unjust. It seemed to

her a terrible thing to have happened. All her life she had known him as gentle and kind and wise. And just at this moment, when she wanted him so passionately to go on being the same, he had cruelly mistaken Mark's silliness for cowardice.

In the sharpness of her misery, Mary noticed the tiniest details of the things about her. A snowflake had swung slowly down through the sheltered stillness on the seaward side of the Marram Hills. She watched it settle on the outstretched point of a dead starfish at her feet. The topmost dead pods on the bush lupin stem rattled as she stirred. Out to sea the waves looked like the backs of hippopotamuses, rounded and solid and shiny.

"Goodness," she thought, with half her mind. "I've never seen them look like that before."

She shivered.

It was not only her father's anger that upset her so much. Mary was too honest to deceive herself about that. It was what he had said in his anger.

"I can never forgive you for being a coward."

What if these terrible words, said unjustly and in anger to Mark, had been addressed quietly and with justice to herself?

Mary saw herself as the most horrible coward. She was afraid of the sight of blood and of sudden, loud noises and of people moving about in the dark. When she was younger, before she had gone away to school, she had been able to laugh about it all with Myrtle.

"It's cos yew read all them books," Myrtle had said. "Yew stop readin' and yew won't go lookin' for mad women under yer bed every night or expectin' that Mr. Hyde yew were talkin' of to come jumpin' out on yer behind the coalhouse door."

But Mary had not been able to stop reading, and she had continued to be afraid. She was afraid of the dentist, afraid

of car accidents and people lying hurt in the road, and—
worst of all—she was afraid of showing that she was afraid.
No one could really love a coward, and she longed very
much for the people whom she knew to go on loving her
still.

The Cottage by the Gap

Up in the Scottish Highlands, early that afternoon, the gale sliced the tops off the trees. The winds mowed through the forest plantations, snapping and smashing and uprooting the pines.

As she sat on the Norfolk shore, Mary saw a man, half a mile away, walking slowly down the coast toward her. He was dragging a sack and stopping every now and again to pick up something from the sand.

"I know who it is," she thought, smiling to herself.

It was Jim Foulger, out coaling. As he stooped to pick up the dull, rounded pieces of coal that the sea washed up, she noticed how clumsily he used his injured arm.

Mary knew all about that arm. She had answered the ring at the surgery door the night Jim shot away half his hand. She would never forget that night. As he leaned against the wall, he kept scuffling one foot backward and forward on the step, his whole body hunched up in the shadow.

"What's the matter, Jim?" she had asked. "What's the matter?"

He was muttering and sighing to himself.

"Git yer dad, Miss Mary. Git yer dad. Don't yew look at me, Miss Mary."

But Mary had already seen his left hand. He was trying to

hold it up with his right hand, and yet to hide it from her eyes. Blood was gushing out where his first and second fingers should have been. Mary had given a little cry. She would have fainted or done something disgraceful had she not seen Jim's face first. It was white and pleading like a hurt child's. She had grasped the wrist of the injured hand, and, having seen that her thumb was in the right place to stop the flow of blood, as her mother had once taught her, she had shouted for her father to come.

Father had hushed it all up. Jim had been out poaching in Sir Bartlett's woods, over by Herringford Mill, and the trigger of his gun had got jammed in a twig. Three miles he had walked, clutching his arm.

As the distance between them shortened, Mary and Jim Foulger gave each other a screwed-up, secret little smile. They always met like this. Neither of them had ever referred to the night of Jim's accident again.

"Yer grown a fine mauther, Miss Mary," the old man shouted. "Haven't sin yew since the summer. Will yer come home and see Hepzie? She don't git out much now, cos of 'er arthritis. It 'ud mek her reel happy." Mary grinned and nodded, and Jim turned to walk slowly up the coast with her toward Reedsmere Gap.

The Foulgers lived in a little shingle cottage with a reed-thatched roof, a hundred yards north of the Gap on the landward side of the Marram Hills. It stood on half an acre of ground a little raised above the surrounding marsh, so that in the usual winter floods both the cottage and its garden stood dry and snug above the water.

"It's nice and private like," Hepzie used to say. "Yew can see yer visitors in winter walking along the dune toward yew, near a mile away."

As far as Mary knew, the Foulgers never had visitors in winter, but she saw what Hepzie meant.

In high summer it was a different matter. There was a lane fifty yards inland from the edge of Reedsmere Broad that was completely hidden by rushes and reeds, growing six feet high and more on either side. When they were younger, Mark and Mary used to come silently down this lane and then jump out on Hepzie as she was stooping over her strawberry bed or planting out her winter greens. It was a grand lane for stalking.

The wind was now so high that it roared in the open sky. Mary's hair jumped and swirled and slapped so hard about her head that she kept getting bits in her eyes and mouth. Jim leaned his old body against the gusts and shoved himself forward as though he were pushing a heavy barrow. Conversation was impossible.

When they came to the Gap, where the cow had stood, Jim kicked his foot against the splitting sandbag wall.

"They'll hev to do something about this if we're not to hev the sea in agin," he grunted.

Hepzie's cottage was a haven of peace after the tumult outside. And there sat Hepzie herself, a little fatter and a little older, knitting away at a fisherman's long sock in oiled white wool.

"Oh, Hepzie, you've got our shawl on!" cried Mary in delight. "And your locket too!"

She ran forward and put her arms around the old woman.

With Hepzie, Mary forgot the bottled-up, awkward feeling that had come upon her so uncomfortably in the last few months. With Hepzie one was just oneself.

There was a strong smell of mothballs in the room.

"Why, Hepzie, you've only just taken it out of the trunk under your bed!" She laughed. "How did you know I was coming?"

"That's telling, Miss Mary," Hepzie replied, but as she spoke she lifted her eyes to the little square window on the right of the hearth. Mary glanced too. Through its panes she saw the long stretch of sand dune running south, with the tufts of long, dead marram grass tossing in the wind. She and Jim must have been visible to Hepzie for the last ten minutes.

"And Hepzie, you've got your lovely locket on, too!" exclaimed Mary again, overcome with delight to find everything as she had always remembered it.

She fingered the round little seed pearls set in its edge, as she had fingered them a thousand times before.

"Here yew are, me luv," smiled the old woman, taking it off over her head. "Sit down and hev your play with it, while Jim gits us a cup of tea."

On the front was the name *Annie* written in gold letters across the blue enamel. On the back were the words *Amor vincit omnia*. If you put a long thumb nail in the crack along the side, the locket opened, and inside under two glass ovals were two locks of hair, one fair and curly, the other black and straight. Who Annie was, Hepzie did not know; nor did she know to whom the hair had belonged.

"It must have been your mother or grandmother," Mary had once suggested.

But the old woman had shaken her head. "No, luv, we've bin Hepzibahs, mother and daughter, right back to Boney's time."

The locket was a complete mystery.

"Whoever Annie was, the boy weren't no local boy," Hepzie had once announced.

"Oh, Hepzie, why not?"

"Cos of his hair, of course. Hev you ever seen a black-headed boy round here, Miss Mary? Unless, of course, he were a foreigner from the shires. All us Norfolk folk hev yellow hair, or red." Then Hepzie had laughed. "You should hev seen me Jim in the old days! There never was such a carroty one!"

Jim was clumsy in the house. He could carry things comfortably only in his right hand, so as he moved about the room and put the kettle on the hearth, he walked right side foremost as though he were an agile kind of crab. But he was quick and willing. As he sidled about he kept throwing out remarks.

"It's one of them high tides, tonight," he grunted. "Shouldn't wonder it 'ud just come licking up to the Gap."

As he clattered the cups down on the table any how, Hepzie tidied them straight.

"And it's a nor'wester, too," he continued. "That's the flood wind, Mother."

"They'll be having trouble up at King's Lynn, maybe, is that what yer thinkin', Jim?"

"Yes, and up the Yare and the Waveney, and up all them rivers, right down to the Thames."

Mary looked puzzled.

"I never can understand why a north*west* wind brings floods," she said. "I should have thought that the west wind would have blown them away."

"Ah, but it's got to hev the north in it too, Miss Mary," replied Jim. "Yew see, it's like this. The north wind blows the water in the sea down the coast, slap up against the coast of Holland. It can't git out quick enough into the Channel through them Dover Straits, along o' them bein' so narrow. And the water piles up high in the North Sea. Got that?"

"Yes, I've got that."

"Then we've got them rivers, the Ouse up at King's Lynn, the Yare, the Bure, and the Waveney. Well, them valleys are full of flood water at this time of the year. Just think of our soggy marshes round here. Why, miss, come to the winder and look at that marsh atween yer house and this."

Mary looked. She knew the scene as well as Jim. Long ribbons of water stretched across the land, bright for the moment in a gleam of winter sunlight.

"Now with the ebb tide, miss, and helped with the west wind, all that water ought to go drainin' out to sea."

"Yes, I know it ought."

"But it can't. The sea's all piled up. It's like a great wall. The water that's trying to flow down them rivers meets a great wall of water in the sea. It can't git through. Then what happens?"

"It bursts out sideways," exclaimed Mary, suddenly seeing the answer to her question.

"That's it, me mauther; it bursts out sideways over the marshes, high up them river valleys. And then we hev acres and acres of grazing land flooded."

Hepzie, somewhat surprisingly, suddenly burst out laughing.

"D'yew remember the time, Jim, yew and I rowed over the dam from Gillingham to Beccles, that time we were staying with yer sister Florrie? That's what we did, luv, we rowed over that dam with the telegraph poles on either side, and that raised foot path all under water beside us."

Jim laughed too.

"And then we rowed about in someone's orchard under them apple trees. And yew got yer het caught in one of them twigs. You should've seen that het, miss. Gorgeous it was. Nothing like it now. All wax cherries and bits of wool flowers."

"G'arn with yew, Jim."

Mary had seldom seen them laugh so much together.

"Were you just married then?" she asked shyly.

"That's it, luv," replied Hepzie. "Nineteen twelve it was, and me and Jim had just been wed. It's a long time ago."

Mary remembered that moment in the little cottage many times during the coming week. It was such a natural, happy moment—Jim and Hepzie laughing over Hepzie's hat stuck in the apple tree, and the firelight winking in Hepzie's china ornaments in the corner cupboard. The wind banging on the window panes only made it the more precious, perhaps just because it allowed it to be so brief.

Suddenly a great blast shook the cottage and crashed something large, metallic, and hollow against the back door. The noise was appalling.

"Bless my soul, Hepzie!" exclaimed Jim when he had un-latched the door. "It's yer washtub blown clean out of the wash house. Whatever next!"

He brought it in and put it on the table.

He suddenly looked serious.

"With a wind like this there's no knowin' what'll happen."

Home

Mary went home along the marsh lane. By keeping to the top of the ruts made by the reed cutter's carts, she avoided the worst of the mud. The wind was flattening the last thin fringe of reeds beside her path, and over their swaying, feathery tops she saw the full expanse of Reedsmere Broad, shining in the sunlight.

How beautiful it was! Such sudden, unexpected beauty! Far away across the Broad, the last-year stems of the willow trees shone red and yellow in the light; and the dry reeds in the reed bed opposite glowed golden-brown like ripe corn. Their feathery tops plumed gray and soft. As the wind tore across the surface of the Broad, the water puckered up in dark little waves, which set the reed beds swaying gently up and down. Seagulls were scattered about the lower air just above the level of the water. They screeched as they struggled up the wind.

"They can't manage it any more than I can," she said to herself as she watched them trying to make for their feeding ground on the mud flat to the north.

Mary had left her cares behind her, as she so often did after a visit to the Foulgers; and now, with the glow of the wind in her cheeks, and the last chance sunlight of this winter's day lighting the gray flintwork of Reedsmere Church and the rich pantiles and brickwork of the Pickerel Inn and suddenly glorifying the marsh and the willows and the Broad, she felt her heart fill with love for the world she knew.

And then, because along this flat east coast half the world means the sky, Mary turned her eyes upward. The sun would set in another hour; the western end of the village already lay deep in shade. Above her the sky rose yellowish-green, streaked weirdly with black and gold—black with the wind-torn clouds, and gold where the sun caught their western flanks. It was a racing, swirling scene, black and gold and yellowish-green—changing and parting—the clouds now drawn out into thin ribbons, now massed in dark billowing folds.

As she was passing the reed stack, Mark suddenly jumped out on her.

"Boo on you, Mooney!"

He caught her around the waist, and they rolled over together on a pile of dry, snapping reed stems.

Mary gazed at him doubtfully as they sat up covered with broken bits of reed.

"Wasn't it awful?" she asked.

Mark began to laugh.

"You were a silly ass to go bolting out of the house like that."

"Why, what happened?"

"Nothing."

"Nothing? What do you mean?"

"Well, after you dashed away, Dad sat and looked puzzled for a bit. Then he said he thought he'd made a mistake, and that what I'd told him was probably quite right."

"Quite right?"

"That Dotty Dick's cottage *did* look a dreadful sort of mess, and that it was disgraceful nowadays that anyone should be living in such a hole."

"And?"

"And then he said he thought that if he'd been a boy he might have done the same as me."

"Done what?"

"Thought that no one could possibly live in such a tumble-down place, and that it was rather fun to lam a stone through that rotten old glass."

"And then what did he say?"

"That he believed I hadn't failed to tell him because I was afraid but just because I was a stupid ass."

"Oh, I'm so glad," sighed Mary.

"Well, it wasn't as good as all that," Mark said ruefully. "Mum got going then."

"What did *she* say?"

"She said I was horribly untidy and thoughtless and un-disciplined—and why hadn't I scrubbed my fingernails before coming to lunch? Then she said I ought to start pulling up my shoes."

"Socks, silly."

"All right, socks. But she meant shoes. Dad tumbled over my boots on the step this morning."

"Who's going to pay for the glass?"

"We're going shares, Dad and me. Dad got Tim Wright to put in a new pane this morning."

"Oh, I'm so glad it's all right again." Mary sighed, as a great wave of relief swept through her.

They lay back for a minute with their backs against the sheaves of reeds, gazing out across the water winking in the evening light. On the far side of the Broad the air was full of straw.

"Look." Mark laughed. "The wind's got into the Catch-poles' stack."

When they returned home, they found their mother sitting in the drawing room, sewing on name tapes. Mark ran through to the playroom to add an owl's pellet, which he had just picked up, to the other treasures in his museum; and Mary and her mother were left alone.

"I'm so glad you've come back, darling. You worry me when you take flight like that."

Mary kissed the top of her mother's head and sat down on the arm of her chair.

It was wonderfully quiet and warm, after the buffeting of the wind outside—wonderfully peaceful and comforting, sitting there watching her mother sew, after the family storm at lunch.

"Aren't you terribly hungry?" asked her mother at last.

Mary could not help laughing. Whenever she had one of her fits of despair, her mother's first concern was to fill her up with food.

"But you rushed off without eating any pudding."

"I don't expect you finished yours, did you, Mother?"

The two looked at each other and smiled.

"Let's open the last pot of honey for tea," suggested Mrs. Vaughan.

The drawing room was a beautiful room. Two French windows opened west into the rock garden, and a large bay window overlooked the quay and the Broad to the north. It was a room in which glancing shadows of birds and clouds sped along the pictures, and in which you never forgot for a moment that you were near open spaces and reeds and water. In sunny weather the reflection of the Broad shimmered on the ceiling by the north window, and the three-paneled mirror over the fireplace reflected the green foliage and the flowers in the garden outside.

That stormy winter dusk, Mary and her mother sat for a moment looking at the last light streaking the wind-torn rags of the clouds.

Then Mrs. Vaughan shivered suddenly as though she had read their future in the sky.

"Draw the curtain, Mary," she said. "And let's make toast."

Father came home with snowflakes glistening in his eye-brows and his thick hair tossed and ruffled by the wind. He sat down in his chair by the fire, and, in leaning forward to catch its warmth, he rested his hand on Mary's shoulder, as she knelt there toasting the slices of bread. Nothing more! But it was enough. Mary could read the message through the touch of his hand.

"It's all right," he was saying. "I know what you were thinking when you dashed out of the room at lunch. But it's all right. Don't worry."

Mary turned her fire-flushed face toward him and smiled.

"Shall I wipe your glasses?" she asked. "They're all misty with snow and rain."

Mother came in with the tea tray.

"The clematis has just blown loose from the wall," she said. "I'll have to nail it up again tomorrow."

"It's a terrible night," said Dr. Vaughan, putting on his glasses again. "There's a tree down across the Herringford Road."

"Jim Foulger says it's the flood wind, Father."

"Well that's nice and cheerful of him! Jim's one of those people who love to prophesy doom."

"It doesn't make our drive to Norwich sound any more pleasant," sighed Mrs. Vaughan.

"To Norwich?"

"Yes, darling. Father and I are dining tonight with old Mr. Paget in the Close."

"I didn't know."

"Well, you ought to listen, Mooney," threw in Mark, looking up from his copy of *Eagle*. "Mum's told us about it at least twice this week."

"I've made a coffee mocha pudding for your supper, to cheer you both up," said Mrs. Vaughan. "It's in the pantry."

When their parents came into the drawing room to say good-bye, Mary was tuning her violin, and Mark was sitting on the floor, taking his father's microscope out of its case.

"We'll just listen to the weather forecast before we go," said Dr. Vaughan, switching on the radio.

"That clock is six minutes slow, you know," said Mark.

He was right. The news had already begun, and they came into the middle of it.

". . . was on her beam ends," came the announcer's voice, "and he gave the order to abandon ship. R.A.F. planes dropped lifesaving equipment, and tonight flares were dropped where survivors were seen in the water. Reports about the rescue work are still coming in."

"Gosh, Dad, there's been a wreck!" exclaimed Mark.

"Sh! Sh!" they all said.

"The full force of the gales," continued the announcer, "is being felt in the extreme north of Scotland. The crew of the seven-thousand-ton steamer *Clan Macquarrie* were rescued after she had gone aground off the Butt of Lewis . . . All sea and air services there are at a standstill. Many telephones in Scotland are out of action, and some districts are without electricity because trees have been blown across overhead cables. In Liverpool, a man was killed and three people injured when a wooden tram shelter was blown down . . ."

"It's all in the north and west," observed Father.

"Sh, dear. Let's listen," said Mother.

"Gales are officially forecast for nearly all districts of the British Isles tonight; in the north they will be severe. But winds will die down slowly during the night and tomorrow. Squally showers of rain or snow will occur in most districts, with hail in places. . . . Two new high-speed jet aircraft are to be built in the United Kingdom by . . ."

Father switched off.

"There's no flood warning, Kitty," he smiled, "and no particular threat to our little bit of Norfolk."

Mark and Mary saw their parents to the car.

"Ring up Canon Crowfoot, if you're worried about anything, darlings," called out their mother. "Do you remember his number?"

"Reedsmere twenty-six," shouted Mark, as he ran back quickly to inspect his owl's pellet under the microscope.

The wind still chased around the house.

Mary put up the music stand and practiced Mayas' Study in E Minor, one of the pieces for the examination she was taking at the end of the coming term. Then she gave herself up to pleasure and played the opening movement of Beethoven's Sonata in D.

Mark, heedless of finer feelings, kept shouting out his discoveries.

"Gosh! Here's a bit of mouse's tooth!"

"Shut up!" hissed Mary through her teeth.

"And lots of chewed-up feathers. Sparrows, I think."

But, now that she was fairly launched, away soared Mary and Beethoven, triumphant over the wind outside and the grisly recital of the owl's last meals within.

Just after seven, they drifted into the kitchen, only faintly hungry, but curious to inspect their favorite pudding awaiting them in the pantry.

Back in the drawing room twenty minutes later, they felt a little aimless and unsettled. Mark sprawled on the hearthrug and read his copy of *Eagle* for the third time. Mary rummaged halfheartedly through her mother's work basket to see if she had collected any pretty buttons or curious-looking buckles lately.

The wind had died for the moment, and the night was still. But Mary suddenly looked up, startled. Out of the corner of her eye she had caught sight of something odd and dark on the floor.

"Mark!" she exclaimed. "Someone has spilled a whole lot of water by the window!"

They both ran to look at the huge puddle.

"It's coming in from outside!"

Mary drew the curtains, and they peered out into the darkness.

"Heavens!" said Mark, with a great lump in his throat.

The garden, as far as they could see, was one large sheet of water.

January 31—Night

"How silently it has come!" murmured Mary, mesmerized by the wonder outside.

Little waves were lapping across a lake that only an hour ago had been the tennis lawn. Desert islands, that were the topmost peaks of Mrs. Vaughan's rock garden, stood up defiantly against the rising water. Soon they, too, would be submerged.

"Oh, Mark!" cried Mary, suddenly awake to the danger of what she saw. "Father! Mother! What will have happened to them? They'll have been caught in this on their way to Norwich!"

"No they won't, silly. They'll be in Norwich already. It's half-past seven. They were dining at seven. That's why they started so early."

They continued to stand there watching the islands disappear one by one. Then, because their feet were getting wet, they looked down at the puddle beside them. It had trebled in size and was now stretching a long arm under the sofa.

"Mum'll hate this mess it's making," said Mark.

Mark's concern was as astonishing as everything else that had happened in the last few minutes. It jolted Mary into action.

"Let's pull up the hearthrug."

They pulled up the hearthrug and put it on the table. Then they took out the bottom shelf of books in the bookcase—heavy books they were—fifteen volumes of Chambers' Encyclopaedia and all Mother's art books. But when they had put them safe and dry on the table, they realized that this was not nearly enough. The water was now covering the whole floor; it had risen to the bottom of the pleated frills of the loose covers on the chairs.

"It's no good, Mark. We'll have to carry them upstairs. The whole room may be under water soon."

They worked methodically and sensibly.

Panting and a little exhausted, having carried the hearthrug, the piano stool, Mother's work basket, Father's microscope, the precious record player and the box of long-playing records, and then all the books from the second and third shelves up to the landing above, they stood for a moment trying to think what their parents would have done next.

"I think we ought to loop up those long curtains," said Mary. "The bottoms are wet, but it will save the rest of them."

They gazed mournfully at the sofa and two big armchairs. They knew that they were far too heavy for them to move. And the piano! There was nothing they could do about the piano.

The water was now creeping through into the passage and the other downstairs rooms. In the kitchen it was already two inches deep.

"Help me get the books out of the playroom, Mary, quick."

It was while they were upstairs putting down the last bundle—the Beatrix Potter and *Orlando* books beloved in early childhood—that all the lights went out.

Mary gave a gasp. She had always hated the dark. Mark knew this. He reached out clumsily and squeezed her arm.

"It'll be all right, Mooney. I know it will."

"I know it will, too, Mark. It was just the surprise of it."

They stood in the darkness holding hands for a moment, and then Mary's anxious mind found another care.

"Do you think we ought to ring up Canon Crowfoot and tell him we're quite safe? He may worry."

They crept downstairs to the telephone, and splashed their way to their father's surgery. Mark lifted the receiver to get the operator. They waited half a minute in silence.

"There's not a sound. The line must be cut."

The two stood close to each other shivering a little, not frightened about their own safety, but bewildered at the extraordinary things that were happening in their own very ordinary little world.

"Let's see if we can find that funny flashlight Father puts on his head to see down people's throats," suggested Mark. "One can't do anything sensible without some light."

They rummaged about blindly in the drawers among pads of Health Ministry forms and sample packets of pills, till they at last unearthed it. Mark put it over his head and shone a beam full into Mary's face.

"You look awfully cold," he said.

"My feet are so beastly wet."

"Let's go and get our Wellington boots, carry them up-stairs, and then change into something dry."

Mark's extreme sense of the practical was wonderfully comforting.

It was while they were sitting on the floor in Mark's bedroom, groping their way into dry clothes, that Mary made her horrible discovery.

She had scratched her finger that afternoon on a sharp, dead lupin stem, and now as she pulled off her wet sock it began to sting.

"It's salt, Mark! It's salt!"

"What's salt?"

"The water."

They both licked their wet hands. There was no doubt about it. The flood that had covered their garden and was rising every minute in the downstairs rooms was sea water!

"It's broken through the Gap," she whispered. "The sea has broken through the Gap."

Mary's mind darted back to that afternoon. She saw Jim kicking at the rotten sandbags in Reedsmere Gap. She saw old Hepzie, stout and arthritic, knitting in her chair beside the fire. She heard again the crash of the washtub against the cottage door.

"Mark!" she shouted. "Hepzie and Jim! We must *do* something. Their cottage is right down by the sea—far lower than our house. The water must be right up their stairs and in their bedroom. Oh, Mark, what *can* we do?"

They pulled on their dry socks, their minds darting backward and forward, chasing impossible ideas.

"I know!" said Mark at last.

He dashed to his bedroom window and looked out across the flooded garden to the boat house.

"I'll put on Dad's salmon-fishing boots. They're in the attic. I saw them yesterday. Then I'll get to the boat house and bring *Donovan* back to you."

"But the boat's stuck up on those boxes."

"It'll have floated off in this."

"And the boat-house doors. You'll never get them open. We can't do it by ourselves at high tide. You know we can't."

"But Mary, I won't come out by the Broad. I'll float the boat out backward through the garden. You'll see."

Mark had clattered off downstairs in the fishing boots. They were much too large for him, their top flaps almost reaching to his ribs. And then Mary ran to the bedroom window and opened it to watch him wade across the garden.

"Keep to the path," she shouted. "It's higher and firmer."

His movements were slow, for the water was heavy to

push against. She watched Father's flashlight, which he was still wearing around his head, swing slowly from right to left as he put down his feet. And then, after a few minutes, it disappeared inside the boat house.

Meanwhile, as the warmth crept down her dry socks inside her Wellingtons, Mary began to feel far braver. She noted the fact with interest.

Then she groped her way to the chest of drawers in her bedroom and picked out three thick jumpers, which she put on, one on top of the other. And then she took out her thick yellow school scarf and tied it in a turban round her head with one end loose, trailing down over her shoulder. She had never worn it like this before, but it made her feel full of dash and valor—like the picture of Lord Byron setting out to free the Greeks from the Turks.

"I expect other people feel like that about the cold, too," she thought.

And she crept back into Mark's room, feeling her way with her hands along the wall. Then she took his heavy football sweater out of the trunk his mother had packed so neatly that morning, and took out his school scarf, too. She knew them both by their feel. And then she crept down the stairs, waded through the drawing room, and waited for Mark's return by the open French window.

"Oh, hurry! Hurry!" she kept muttering to herself.

She saw so clearly the terrible danger in which the Foulgers lay, and as she looked across the desolate drawing room, faintly lit by the dying fire, she thought with pain of all the precious minutes she and Mark wasted trying to save their treasures.

A great sob rose up in her throat and got stuck there.

"We've been doing all the selfish unchristian things Canon Crowfoot is always telling us not to do," she thought. "We've been thinking about things instead of people. We've been

trying to save our books and the carpet and Father's microscope. And all the time Hepzie and Jim are helpless out there
in the path of the sea."

What must be happening to the old couple was too appalling to think about.

Meanwhile Mark was hardly less miserable. As he waded
slowly across the heavy water, he thought to himself.

"The oarlocks! The oarlocks! Please God, make me have
left them where I ought to have left them."

Mark knew how untidy he was. He never put anything
away.

"If I've been careless and left them on the boat-house floor
instead of hanging from the hook on the wall, we shan't be
able to use the boat. Hepzie and Jim will both be drowned,
and it'll be all my fault."

He reached the boat house in a fever of fear. He shone his
flashlight around the wall. There they were! The oarlocks
glinted brightly back at him.

Mark lifted the oars from the slots along the walls, carried
the rudder and put it into the rowboat, and pushed and
tugged till the boat slowly freed itself from the boxes. He
jumped in, pushed out hard against the boat-house wall with
an oar, and was out in the garden.

As the rowboat approached the French windows, it
brought behind it the forked wave of its wash. Mary grasped
the side of the boat to steady it, and the wave swept on into
the room and drowned the fire. It went out with a hiss—an
eerie and uncomfortable signal that they had finished for that
night with fires and warmth and home.

Mary seized her violin in its case from the top of the piano
and stepped into the boat. Mark shone his light on her
turban.

"You look awfully odd in that."

"It's warm."

"I wish I had my scarf, too."

"I've got it here, and your pullover."

Mark dashed back into the house, ran halfway up the stairs, changed out of the dangerously heavy fishing boots into his lighter Wellingtons, put on his pullover and scarf, and returned to the boat with the rugger ball his father had given him for Christmas.

As they put their treasures in the center of the boat, neither commented on the other's oddness. They understood. Mary with infinite patience and delicacy threaded the two prongs of the rudder through the tiny steel hoops at the stern of the boat—a feat Mark was always too clumsy to perform for himself—and they set out.

Out of the shelter of the house, the wind suddenly caught at them. It howled and roared over the great sweep of the waters, tossing and flattening the tops of the willows, shrieking in the elms, and blowing the water into waves, which spanked and slapped against the bow of the boat. Rags of the storm clouds still streamed south across the sky; Mary could see them faintly white against the farther black.

Mark rowed with the strength and skill of a man. He had been managing a boat single-handed for four years, since he was seven. Mary clutched at the rudder ropes and peered into the swirling darkness ahead.

They were just over Mother's favorite herbaceous border. In a second they would be out on Reedsmere Broad.

"Row with your right, Mark," she shouted. "I'm going to turn down toward the sea."

She pulled hard on the right rudder rope, and the boat lurched broadside on to the wind. With the force of the gale it was driven sideways over the marsh beside their garden. Mark stood up to the oars and threw the whole weight of his body into his backward pull, and slowly the boat edged its way east toward the end of the Broad.

"Wouldn't it be better if we pulled into the center of the Broad?" he yelled at her through the wind. "These reeds and rushes keep fouling my left oar."

Mary looked at the water in the center of the Broad. A great swirl of angry waters was hurtling inland with the speed of a mountain torrent.

"No," she yelled back. "The sea is sweeping straight down the middle of it."

They kept to the edge of the flood. They were on the landward side of the lane Mary had walked along that afternoon. Ten yards on their left they passed the topmost two feet of the reed stack behind which Mark had hidden.

"Heavens! Mary, the flood must be at least seven feet deep here. Look at the stack!"

Mary nodded. She was thinking of something far more important. The Foulgers' cottage lay on the far side of that swirling inrush of sea. If they were to save Hepzie and Jim they would have to cross it.

"Mark, we've got to cross that sea water sometime. How do we do it?"

Mark gave two great strokes with the oars before he answered.

"I think we row right up under the Marram Hills," he shouted back. "Turn round in the shelter there, and then cross it diagonally. What do you think?"

Mary nodded.

"The sea will help us, and we can spend all our time

steering. With luck we ought to land up on the other side, somewhere near the cottage."

The nearer they rowed to the dark line of the Marram Hills, the louder the sea roared in their ears. The waves pounded on the shore again and again and again.

"Oh, please stop. Please, please stop. Just for a minute," whimpered a very small girl somewhere inside Mary's head.

The wind tore across the sky. It was bitterly cold. *Donovan* was about opposite the Foulgers' cottage by now, but as they peered over the cresting torrent at the darkness beyond, they could see neither a lighted window nor even the dark outline of the cottage against the distant flood.

"Oh, surely it can't have been washed away," gasped Mary to herself.

The thought of Hepzie, crippled with arthritis, and Jim, with his maimed hand, struggling in that icy swirl of water was so horrible that she felt quite dizzy with terror.

"Mary, don't shut your eyes like that," shouted Mark. "We've got to think."

There was a note of alarm in his voice. Mary opened her eyes and gathered her courage to herself. They were holding on to tufts of marram grass three-quarters of the way up the Marram Hill. Together they looked at the great wall of water surging through the gap. It was impossible for their rowboat, sturdy and squat though it was, to live in that raging sea.

As they watched, a ship's mast suddenly reared up through the Gap and tossed and tumbled landward into the Broad. They both watched it disappearing under the water and then shooting up again as it hurtled past.

"The poor ships at sea!" gulped Mary.

But Mark was comparing the fate of the mast with the probable fate of the rowboat should they venture to cross the sea race.

"I was wrong," he said miserably. "We ought to have

crossed it further inland where it has had a chance to fan out. I'm going to row back to the reed stack and try to cross there."

Mark gritted his teeth, and silently pulled back over the marsh; the incoming spring tide bore them along with magic speed.

At the reed stack Mary took control. Through the gloom she had seen Mark's taut gray face.

"It wasn't your fault that you thought up the wrong plan, Mark. It was my fault, too."

As they held on to the stack, clutching with tense fingers at the reeds, they looked across the broad stretch of swirling waters.

"I'm going to pull out the rudder, Mark, and sit beside you on the seat. I'll take the right oar. You've rowed nearly a mile and you're tired. It's the right oar that has got to get us across."

Mark nodded but did not move.

"Shove over," she said, almost sharply.

They sat beside each other in the old boat as they had sat so often on sunny, happy, summer days, when each had tried to row harder than the other, and the boat had jerked briskly, now left, now right, across the gentle Broad.

"Now," said Mary. "When you see that we are getting too broadside on to the race, you've got to pull like blazes, and I'll backwater. But if things work out as I think they'll work out, the sweep of the sea and me rowing with the right oar ought to get us across."

They put the violin and the rugger ball under the stern seat, clenched their teeth, and set out. At first it was as Mary had thought. Mary rowing, and the water streaming inland, carried the boat diagonally across the race. Halfway across, however, a sudden swirl caught at the stern of the boat and turned it completely around.

"We'll have to reverse everything," yelled Mark.

Mark began to backwater with terrific strength—and in some way that they were never quite able to explain afterwards, the rowboat slid stern first into the quieter waters on the north side of Reedsmere Broad.

"We've done it!" They grinned at each other.

Then, still sitting side by side, they pulled with the long, hard, even strokes their father had taught them, toward the Foulgers' cottage and the Marram Hills.

Jim was cutting a hole through the reed thatch with Hepzie's carving knife when they at last reached the darkened cottage. He had got his head and shoulders out.

"It's the children, Hepzie!" he shouted back down the hole. "It's the children, luv."

"Oh, Jim, oh, Hepzie, we're so glad you're all right," they both yelled back.

They clutched at the eaves of the thatch with their hands. Jim was working at his hole on a slope of roof about three feet above them.

"Can't get Mother out through the winder," he explained. "You're too fat, ain't yew, Mother?"

They could hear Hepzie laughing in the bedroom inside. Suddenly they all started laughing. Oh, the relief of knowing that they were both alive!

Mark scrambled up the thatch to help tear away at the hole with his hands. Meanwhile Mary sidled the boat carefully around to the little bedroom window. She could see Hepzie sitting on the bed, still wrapped in their woolen shawl, and she saw Jim's legs as he stood on a chair, reaching up through the ceiling. Mary tapped on the glass, and Hepzie, all smiles moved slowly to the window and opened it.

"There's my treasure," she whispered. "There's my treasure."

Mary felt that her face was wet with tears.

"It's awfully cold, Hepzie dear," she whispered back. "Wrap yourself up in all the coats you've got, and when Jim and Mark have made that hole bigger we'll row you somewhere safe."

How they got Hepzie out through that hole in the roof no one could quite say afterward. Jim moved the bed under the hole, and then put a chair on top of the bed. And somehow, with pulls and heaves from the three of them, the old woman got herself up on to the thatch and let herself slide slowly down into the boat.

Jim had caught up their patchwork eiderdown before they left the cottage, and he wrapped up Hepzie and Mary in it in the stern of the boat, took the right oar, and then settled himself down beside Mark.

"Now, my hearties," he laughed. "Where shall we go?"

St. Mary's Church

Almost immediately Jim's question was answered. Through the howling wind and the pounding of the sea came the toll of a church bell. Then came another and another.

They sat motionless, still clutching at the reeds of the Foulgers' thatch, and listened wonderingly to the bell. In a world, mad with the frenzy of the storm, it spoke of calm and sanity, of the Church's ageless orderly ways, of Christmas and Easter and Harvest Festival, of kneeling and praying, and standing and singing. The single bell tolled on and on through the storm.

"Why it's from Reedsmere Church!" exclaimed Jim. "It's parson ringing us to church. Come on, Mark, lad. We'll go."

A moment later the single bell was joined by another, deeper bell. The two began to make a rough pattern. Three short strikes with the first bell, and a long clang from the second.

"Interval of a third," thought Mary. "It's odd! It reminds me of something."

Suddenly Mary felt Hepzie's fat, warm body ripple into laughter under the eiderdown.

"Oh, Jim!" she cried. "Listen to it!"

Jim was laughing too.

"It's the victory sign, that's what it is! It's parson giving us the victory sign."

"What's that?" asked Mark.

The Foulgers looked at him in astonishment.

"Ah, but he's too young to remember, Jim," said Hepzie. "It's the sign we made in the war, luv, when things were bad, and we wanted to remind ourselves that we were going to win."

Jim went on chuckling to himself as he and Mark pulled hard toward Reedsmere Church.

"It en't Tom Mobbs, the verger," he laughed. "He h'en't the wit. It's old parson himself."

"Not so much of the old, Jim Foulger," protested Hepzie. "Why, yew and he were little lads together in old Miss Tufnell's Sunday School. Yew know yew were."

"But what is Canon Crowfoot doing in church at this time of night?" asked Mark. "And who's pulling the other bell with him—or can one pull two at once?"

"Don't know what he's doing, Mark lad," chuckled the old poacher. "But we're going to find out."

As they pulled westward toward the church, the hateful roar of the sea grew fainter and fainter. Mary snuggled against Hepzie and relaxed in a warm comforting smell of mothballs and washed wool. Under the eiderdown she pulled gently at the ropes of the rudder, which they had slid back into its sockets before they left the cottage. She was watching carefully the way the water was behaving on the surface of the Broad; but save for her eyes and her brain and her wind-frozen nose, the whole of her body sat lulled in a beautiful peace.

They were traveling parallel to the sea water, which was still pouring into the Broad in a wide stream of swirling waves. On their crests kept appearing odd bits of spars, pieces of cork, torn netting and, on one occasion, a great yellow, greasy lump of what looked like vaseline.

"That's oil," grunted Jim. "God help the poor devils at sea!"

"But what's that over there?" shouted Mark.

A huge crate was careering inland on the sea swirl, faster than they were able to row on the quieter waters beside it. The box bobbed up and down as it raced wildly past into the gloom ahead.

"A crate of oranges! That's what it looked like!" exclaimed Hepzie. "What ever next!"

"Oranges! Oranges!" Jim stopped rowing and scratched his head. He was trying to catch the tail of a memory out of the past. Then he slapped his leg with his right hand.

"Of course, it's Candlemas! That's what it is! That's why parson's up at the church. And he'll hev all the boys in the choir with him."

"Practicing the Candlemas Carol," joined in Hepzie. "It's just the boys who sing it."

"But why did oranges make you think of Candlemas, Jim?" asked Mary, puzzled.

"Why, Miss Mary, in the old days when Ned Crowfoot and yer grandfer and me were boys, the choir were always given oranges after the Candlemas Carol, leastways we boys were. That's what Ned's doing; he's practicing his carol. Mark, we'd best be putting our backs into this rowing. Parson may be in trouble with this flood and all them little boys. Maybe his victory sign is also a call for help."

They were nearing the outskirts of the village now. They passed the roof of the Pickerel Inn boat house and then the first floor of the Pickerel Inn itself. The water was licking up to the sills of the bedroom window.

"They'll be all right, Jim. Got off in their rowboats, I'll be bound," said Hepzie.

The Pickerel Inn let out boats in summer to excursionists from Norwich and Great Yarmouth and the other coast towns. Mark had seen three of them drawn up on the staithe only two days ago.

"Ay, they'll be all right, Mother. Yew'll niver ketch Ben

Blaza gittin' his feet wet. I 'spect the whole bar-full took off in them boats when the first water came. Dan Ball and Fred Aldis, and the whole lot."

Jim laughed. He was irrepressibly jolly.

"Grown-ups are very odd," thought Mark. "You spill an aquarium of water in the house on ordinary days, and there's the devil to pay. But you take a huge horrid mess like this flood, and it just makes them laugh."

Now the chiming of the two bells was becoming deafening. They seemed almost overhead. They were nearing the church, and they could see the openings of the arched Gothic windows lit with a flickering, soft light from within.

"They've lit the candles, Hepzie," whispered Mary. "Doesn't it look beautiful!"

And then, before they knew it, they were rowing in the churchyard.

"Ship your oar, boy, quick," shouted Jim, "or we'll get them snapped off against them tombstones."

They shipped their oars and handled the boat carefully from one grave to the next, Mary and Hepzie helping as best they could.

"Why, here's yer Great Aunt Amelia's, Jim," exclaimed Hepzie, fending the boat off a particularly large tombstone. One could see her name a foot above the surface of the water.

"Now, steady all," ordered Jim. "We don't want to ram the porch. 'Tisn't seemly."

Quite suddenly there was a sea of excited young faces. All the boy members of Reedsmere Church choir crowded into the porch, squealing with laughter as the wash from the rowboat rolled over the flagstones toward the church door.

"Hullo, Mr. Foulger!" "Hullo, Mrs. Foulger!" "Hullo, Mary!" "Hullo, Mark!' they piped and shouted.

The bells stopped ringing, and they were joined by Canon Crowfoot and Ned Brewster.

Canon Crowfoot towered above his choir, a great, square-jawed, fine, ugly man, like the pictures of Abraham Lincoln. He strode through the boys and waded the three feet to the rise in the gravel path where the boat had grounded.

"Well done, all of you." He smiled. "Welcome to the ark! We're all safe and dry here, aren't we, boys?"

Mary picked up her violin, and Mark clutched his rugger ball, and they both splashed into the porch. Canon Crowfoot seized the painter of the boat and threw it toward Ned Brewster.

"Tie her up, Ned. Yes, to the boot scraper if you like. It's firm enough."

Then, smiling at Hepzie wrapped up in her eiderdown, he said, "Now, Mrs. Foulger, Jim and I are going to give you that four-handed seat we've both been learning about in the Civil Defense class. Come, Jim, take my hands."

The boys had run back into the church to inspect the Vaughans, and the grownups were left alone for a moment in the porch.

"Thank God, Jim, you're safe," murmured the Canon. "I thought it must be all up with you and Mrs. Foulger."

"Well, sir, so it would've been but for the children," replied Hepzie. "They've saved our lives. Rowed all the way down from The Moorings by themselves."

"Where are their parents?"

"Gone to Norwich for the evening," answered Jim.

"Of course, dining with Dr. Paget. I remember now. The children were to ring me if they were worried. Bless me, it's the doctor and his wife that are going to do the worrying when they find out what has happened in Reedsmere tonight."

Mary sat down in the backmost pew of the little church, clutching her violin, and gazed spellbound at the warm, faint glow from the dozen candles on the altar. Their flames looked so fragile as they swayed in the draft, and yet there was an ageless strength in the way that they always righted themselves when the draft had passed, and pointed roof-ward again in steady faith. Their light warmed the ancient walls and set the delicate tracery of the fourteenth-century rood screen in blackest silhouette. Never had the slender pillars looked so invincible, or the arches so strong. After the tumult of the night outside, St. Mary's Church seemed to her a rock, a sure defense.

"I've never seen it like this before," she thought.

Half unconsciously she watched the choirboys still jumping up and down around Mark.

"Why are they so excited?" she asked herself dreamily. "It isn't as though we were strangers. We've known these boys all our lives."

Then she realized why they kept jumping up and down and slapping their sides with their hands. They were cold! She suddenly felt cold herself. A gripping cold from the drafty church was creeping up her from her toes.

"It's splendid that you've brought your rugger ball, Mark," said Canon Crowfoot. "It's just the thing! I want you to organize some kind of game here at the west end—something that keeps you all moving."

Mark had a habit of looking surprised with his ears. At that moment they pricked forward in an expression of astonished disbelief.

"It's all right, Mark," said the Canon. "In olden times they used this church for all sorts of jolly junketings. I'm sure God wouldn't mind you playing a game tonight to keep your-selves warm."

But what game could they play? The west end was almost in darkness, and the space behind the last pew was no more than fifteen feet wide.

"What about Pig in the Middle," suggested Sandy Catchpole, the youngest member of the choir, a whispy pale-faced boy, aged about eight.

"That's a baby's game," jeered Ned Brewster.

"What about Monday, Tuesday," suggested Mary.

"And that's a girl's game," scoffed Mark.

"But don't you see, you old wiseacres," laughed the Canon. "The darkness and the smallness of the space make all the difference! It takes the skill and poise of a rugger international star to play those two games at the west end of St. Mary's in the middle of an electric power cut. Come along, I'll be the first pig."

Laughing, they ran in a scramble to the west end, formed a circle, and pushed their tall parson into the middle. Jim had found two rush-bottomed chairs for himself and Hepzie, which he placed in the central aisle, facing west toward the game. Then he wrapped both of them up in the patchwork eiderdown, and they sat smiling happily, leaning close together to keep each other warm.

At first the Reedsmere boys, not used to a rugger ball, kept dropping it, but as they became accustomed to its oval shape, the ball flew fiercely from side to side of the circle. Now Canon Crowfoot had caught it, and Sandy was pig: then Mary; then Jimmy Bell, the son of the postman; and then Ned Brewster. Warmed to the game, they set the dark corners of the old church ringing to their shouts and laughter, while all across the west end, like a fantastic, moving frieze, the long flickering shadows of their arms and heads played over the whitewashed plaster.

Then suddenly their fun came to an end. A great gust of wind blew in the door leading from the north porch. The rugger ball took a dive through the open space and fell with a splash outside. The boys ran to retrieve it, but stopped dead on the threshold.

"It's risen even more," squeaked Sandy.

"It's right over the porch floor," shouted Ned.

"In another five minutes," thought Mark, "it'll be all over the flagstones where we've been playing."

Canon Crowfoot and Jim stood among the boys, surveying the new inroads of the flood in silence. On the next gust of wind the rugger ball blew back into the church again along the surface of the water. Mark grabbed at it and hugged his wet trophy fiercely to himself.

"Well, boys," said Canon Crowfoot at last, in calm, even tones. "We've all got warm now, so I think we'll return to the chancel and keep our spirits up by singing. Mary, take your violin with you. We'll have a concert. Run along all of you. I want a word with Mr. and Mrs. Foulger."

The choir trooped obediently up to the chancel, leaving the grownups alone.

Off guard, the Canon's face looked gray and worn.

"Things are bad, Jim," he said. "The church is almost the highest point in the village. If we've got water up here what must be happening in Reedsmere Street? All those new houses must be under water. My poor parishioners! Pray God, they are keeping their heads."

"They'll open the Rest Center up at Sir Bartlett Speke's, like in the war. That's what they'll do," said Jim. "That'll be up out of the floods. It's the highest house for miles around."

"What'll we best do with all these poor children, sir?" interrupted Hepzie.

"Until I saw this last rise in the water, Mrs. Foulger, I thought we might sit the flood out here in St. Mary's. Now I think we had better try to take them off by boat."

"Me and Mark can row them up to the big house, three at a time," suggested Jim.

Canon Crowfoot looked at Jim's crippled hand.

"That's too much for you, Jim. Mark's only a child. There must be a heavy swell in the Broad by now, with all sorts of unexpected swirls and eddies. You'll have to keep your wits about you. Take two of the children. The boat won't be so heavy."

"I'll take Ned Brewster and that little chap, Sandy Catchpole," replied Jim. "Ned's a likely sort of lad, and the little 'un can lie quiet at the bottom of the boat. Then Mark and me'll return with help and take the lot of you off. Can't think what Ben Blaza's doing with them Pickerel boats. He oughter been here hours ago."

"Things must be far worse in the village, Jim. He's probably helping there first, and quite right too. We shall be safe here till you return, shan't we, Mrs. Foulger?"

And so it came about on this momentous night that Mark Vaughan and his sister became separated from each other.

"Take care of my ball," said Mark, putting it into Mary's lap as she sat in the chancel.

"Oh, Mark, and do take care of yourself," whispered Mary. "Don't do anything silly."

Her face looked strained.

"I'll be all right, Mooney."

"Must you go?"

"Of course I must. You know old Jim can't manage *Donovan* by himself. Anyhow, Mooney, I *want* to go. It'll be grand to be out on the Broad again. And we'll be back in no time, you'll see."

Off he went, a sturdy, compact, resilient figure, clumping down the aisle in his Wellington boots.

Alone

With the going of Mark, Mary for the first time that night was beside herself with anxiety. She saw in her mind's eye the clumsy *Donovan* caught in a sharp eddy, whirling round and round in the Broad, completely out of control. She saw the great, limitless flood, stealing over the wide Norfolk fields toward Norwich. Soon it would go tumbling down Mousehole Hill into the dip of the city itself. Nobody that she loved was really safe from it—neither Mark battling his way across the Broad nor Father and Mother dining in the Cathedral Close with Dr. Paget.

"Oh, why am I not sharing their dangers with them?" she sobbed silently to herself. "Families should face these things together—not be separated like this."

And then she thought of all the people she loved in Reedsmere—of Myrtle and Mrs. Beamish, of Sally and Jenny, and Miss Cotterel, the schoolmistress. What had happened to them all in this dreadful night?

Gradually she realized that Canon Crowfoot was talking.

"Yes, in the olden days, before little village churches like St. Mary's could afford to buy organs, the choir used to make their own music with fiddles and clarinets and serpents."

"Serpents?" laughed Jim Bell.

"Yes, Jim, curious long, curling wind instruments shaped just like a serpent wriggling across the ground. And a fine deep tone they had, too, according to Mr. Penny."

"Who's he?" asked Mary, interested enough to forget her troubles for a minute.

"He was a member of Mellstock parish choir. You'll meet him when you read Thomas Hardy's *Under the Greenwood Tree*. A fine book for you, when you're a little older, Mary. But come along now, tune up your violin, and the boys and Mrs. Foulger can hear what the Candlemas Carol must have sounded like a hundred and fifty years ago."

Mary took her violin out of its case, tightened her bow, put the chin rest under her chin, and waited for Canon Crowfoot to give her the tuning note of A on the organ.

"It's in G major," said Canon Crowfoot. "I'm afraid it's rather dark for you to read the music."

"I can play it by ear, I think."

She had known the old tune from her earliest childhood, and, until she went to boarding school, she had sung it every February that she could remember.

Effortlessly she played the tune through once. Then the boys sang the first verse to her accompaniment:

> "Down with the rosemary and bays,
> Down with the mistletoe;
> Instead of holly, now upraise
> The greener box, for show."

Now that she felt certain of the notes, her fingers and bow moved mechanically, and her attention wandered:

> "The holly hitherto did sway
> Let box now domineer
> Until the dancing Easter day,
> Or Easter's eve appear."

"Oh, I do wonder what Mother and Father are doing," she thought.

> "Green rushes then, and sweetest bents
> With cooler oaken boughs,
> Come in for comely ornaments
> To readorn the house."

Out of the corner of her eye she saw that water shone blackly at the far end of the aisle.

> "Thus times do shift; thus times do shift;
> Each thing his turn does hold;
> New things succeed; new things succeed.
> As former things grow old."

"Well done!" boomed the Canon from the organ stool. "That sounded splendid."

He rose from his seat and saw the water, too. With an expert eye he measured the height of the two chancel steps and of the single step leading to the altar.

"Fifteen inches! The water can rise another fifteen inches," he thought. "If the worst comes to the worst, I can pack the dozen of them around the altar."

He went over to talk with Hepzie where she sat in his own special seat in the choir stalls.

"It's got an extra comfortable cushion," he had said with a twinkle when he placed her there before the singing of the carol. With her patchwork quilt draped over her shoulders she looked like a benign old bishop in a gay cope.

The boys had moved out of the cramped confines of the choir stalls and were stamping their feet in the aisle of the chancel and swinging their arms around their bodies in a renewed effort to get warm. Three of them ran down the nave to the edge of the water, which had now reached the Foulgers' pew. They stood and contemplated it in silence for a full minute.

"It don't seem to be comin' any further, sir," shouted Jim Bell at last.

"No, sir," shouted another. "Seems to be goin' back a bit."

Mary, in her craving to be nearer her family, was standing on one of the back choir stalls, peering out through the chancel window across the Broad toward their house. She had cleaned the window with her pocket handkerchief and, with her nose pressed hard against the old bluish-tinged glass, she was gazing over the tops of the tombstones at the expanse of water beyond. The longer she looked the more she could see, the wild winter night outside becoming more visible as her eyes forgot the dim candlelight behind her.

Suddenly she saw something which froze her heart with horror. Moving slowly seaward down the Broad drifted an empty rowboat.

Having known its dumpy build from babyhood, there was no mistaking its identity. It was *Donovan.*

"Canon Crowfoot!" she cried. "Come quickly!"

There was so much alarm in her voice that the whole choir ran toward her. In a moment Canon Crowfoot stood on the choir stall beside her.

"It's *Donovan,*" she sobbed. "It's *Donovan.*"

All the boys were clambering on pews or choir stalls to get a view of the boat through the south windows.

"Gosh, what's happened to Ned and Sandy?" gasped one of them.

Suddenly Mary found herself in Hepzie's arms.

"It's all right, me luv. It's all right," the old woman whispered. "Me Jim's bin in some rare scrapes, and so has Mark, but they've always come back all right, h'en't they?"

"But where are they? Why is the boat empty?" sobbed Mary.

A black night of horror closed around her.

"I should never have let him go," she cried.

Canon Crowfoot sat down beside her, took her hands in his, and made her look into his eyes.

"Mary," he said gently. "Mark and Jim and Ned and Sandy

are in the hands of God. Don't take His responsibility to yourself."

"But Father and Mother. How can I ever face them? He is their son."

"And no more precious to them than their daughter."

The Canon looked drawn and gray.

"We must all have courage, my dear. Great courage. And when you are praying for their safety, Mary, remember that it was I who sent them out in that boat."

Then followed a dreadful time. Mary was never to forget it all her life. Hepzie sat beside her, her eyes half closed, withdrawn into some ancient secret world of her own. Perhaps she was praying. Mary did not know. Canon Crowfoot knelt in front of the altar. The boys, shocked into silence, sat huddled in the high embrasures of the Gothic windows, cold and frightened and miserable. The drafts chased round the dark church and blew the candle flames flat, like wind in harvest wheat.

Mary tried to pray herself, but she felt so numbed and shaken that she could not concentrate her thoughts—or rather, she could not tear them away from an appalling memory that now rose like a threatening ghost from the days of her early childhood.

When Mary was about five or six, a party of excursionists from Great Yarmouth had hired two rowboats from the Pickerel Inn. They all wore jaunty white paper caps shaped like those worn by American sailors. Knowing little about the management of oars, they had zigzagged wildly across the Broad, screaming and laughing, and in the middle of the water had rammed the two boats together so hard that a boy had been thrown overboard. Not one of the party could swim, and the boy had been drowned. This was not what

Mary was remembering; she had been told these facts afterward. What haunted her now was the memory of the boy's body, which she had seen laid out on their own lawn. An ordinary sort of boy's body--not unlike Mark's—half covered with a blue bathing towel. It had looked such a pathetic, useless bundle, lying there, quite unlike someone who had laughed and climbed trees and had had to do sums at school.

"What if Mark is now no more than that?" She shuddered.

Suddenly a group of boys in one of the windows stirred.

"There's a man coming up out of the water, sir," shouted one.

"Looks like a spaceman, sir. All covered in rubber, he is," cried another.

"Tall as a tree, sir," shouted a third. "And he's coming into the church."

Through the south door floated a fully inflated, round, rubber dinghy, and behind it, giving it an occasional nudge forward with his shin, strode the tallest man the Reedsmere children had ever seen.

"Hullo, kids!" grinned the young man. Then seeing Canon Crowfoot, who had risen from the altar, he addressed himself to the parson.

"Airman Rod E. Cooper of the United States Army, sir. Can I help you up to the Rest Center with these kids?"

"Good evening, Rod," replied the Canon. "We should all like your help very much."

He eyed the fragile-looking boat doubtfully as it twirled round and round in the few inches of water at the west end of the church.

"Oh, that's safe enough, sir," said Rod, following the Canon's glance. "I've taken ten journeys with her already with folks from the houses in Reedsmere Street. Guess I can take two kids at a time if they sit quiet."

"Have you seen my brother Mark?" asked Mary. "He has fair hair and he's wearing a long green-and-blue striped scarf."

"Hev yer seen Ned Brewster and Sandy Catchpole?" piped a small boy.

"And me mum and dad?" cried another.

Rod shook his head.

"Sorry, kids. I don't know your folks. But there's a number of people sitting on their roofs down the village, and a lot more that've found their way up to Reedsmere Hall."

"Hev you seen my husband, sir?" asked Hepzie. "You can't mistake him. He's only got two fingers to his left hand."

Rod shook his head again."

"Sorry, ma'am. I haven't seen anyone like that."

"Which way did you come, Rod?" asked Canon Crowfoot.

"The flood stops at the lodge gates to Reedsmere Hall, sir. I waded from there down the road toward the church. The beginning and the end of the journey are easy, but in the middle there's a great dip."

"I know, Hollow Bridge!" exclaimed Jimmy Bell.

"Well, by Hollow Bridge the water's so deep it comes right up to my shoulders. That's where you kids'll have to sit quiet."

"Who'll go first, sir?" asked one of the boys.

"I want Mrs. Foulger to go first," replied the Canon. "Then I want Rod to take Mary and one of you smaller boys. Dick Thurgar, what about you? After that we'll get you off two by two. It shouldn't take long."

Twenty minutes later Mary and Dick Thurgar were sitting in the fragile rubber saucer, being skillfully pushed along Church Road by Rod Cooper. Overhead the elms sighed and creaked, and the clouds streamed south, hiding the stars.

"The water's going back into the sea, all right," observed Rod. "See that old stump? Why, when I first came up to the church only its top stuck up out of the water. Now we can see at least a foot of it."

"So that's why *Donovan* was drifting out toward the Gap," thought Mary.

She found herself telling Rod about the boat.

"And it was the right way up, you say?"

Mary nodded.

"Can they all swim?"

"Mark swims wonderfully, and so do Jim and Ned. I don't know about Sandy."

"Sandy can't swim no better than me," put in Dick.

"Well, what you worryin' about, Mary?" grinned Rod. "Boat's not capsized. Three out of four can swim. I'm sure they're O.K."

"Oh, I do hope they are."

They were nearing Hollow Bridge. More and more of Rod had disappeared under the water, so that now he seemed to be pushing it aside with the middle of his chest.

"Tell you what," he puffed, his face on a level with Mary's elbow. "When I've finished at the church, I'll have a look around."

Mary tried to smile her thanks.

"Find them, most like, stuck up on someone's roof."

For one awful moment the water came right up to Rod's neck, and Mary and Dick sat breathless in the little boat wondering if he would ever succeed in getting the two of them and himself to safety.

And now the road was climbing again to the lodge gates, and every second more and more of Rod was to be seen emerging from the water. His strange rubber suit gleamed in the faint light.

"Oh, I'm so glad you're all right," sighed Mary. And then a little later, "Does that thing really keep you dry?" she asked.

"Supposed to." He grinned.

In the distance Mary could see a number of people waiting

on the edge of the flood at the lodge gates. They were peering through the gloom toward Rod and his fragile craft.

"Here he comes!" shouted a man's voice.

"Got your Dick with him, Mrs. Thurgar, and Mary Vaughan too," cried a woman.

"Well done, Rod!" shouted another.

Mary looked up at the tall American who now towered above her.

"Thank you very much, Rod," she said simply. "Will you come to see Father and Mother when this is all over? I know they will want to say thank you, too."

"Sure, Mary," replied Rod. "How do I find your folks?"

"We live on the other side of the Broad. Ask for Doctor Vaughan. Everyone knows where he lives."

"So your father's the doc, eh?" he smiled. "So's mine, back in Illinois."

Now they were right in among the crowd at the lodge gates. Hands helped her out on to the gravel drive. Dick was in his mother's arms. Rod was being pressed to a cup of tea by the lodge keeper's wife, and Mary, eyes searching frantically for Mark and Jim, moved from one dark group to the next, asking the same question over and over again.

"Have you seen my brother Mark? Have you seen Mr. Foulger and my brother Mark?"

No one could remember seeing either of them.

"But don't you fret," Mrs. Thurgar tried to comfort her. "They'll be all right."

"There's a half-dozen boats and more collectin' the families from Reedsmere Street," said another woman. "They'll ·be with them, maybe."

"Don't you worry, don't you worry," came from dark figures whose faces she could not see.

But Mary could not help worrying.

"Have you seen Mr. Foulger and my brother Mark, and Ned Brewster and Sandy Catchpole?" she asked the next group.

"Ned and Sandy?" asked a voice out of the shadows. "Why, they're up at the Hall with their parents. Landed here from a rowboat 'bout an hour back."

"Who else was in the boat?" asked Mary eagerly.

"Can't rightly remember, missy. It put off again quick."

"There's been such a lot o' comin' and goin' tonight, miss," explained a second voice. "It en't easy to remember."

Suddenly her arm was gripped firmly, and she turned to find Mrs. Lindsay of the Women's Voluntary Service.

"Mary, my dear, Mr. Farrow is waiting to take Mrs. Foulger up to the Hall, but she refuses to go without you."

"Where is she?"

"Over there."

Mary walked through the shadows to the lodge keeper's garden. There, waiting to be taken up to the Hall, sat Hepzie, still in her eiderdown, propped up in the lodge keeper's largest wooden wheelbarrow.

"Oh, Hepzie," cried Mary. "I can't leave them like this. I *must* stay here."

"No, luv," replied Hepzie. "There's nothing we can do down here. Yew come up to the Hall. That's where yer mum and yer dad'll be lookin' for yew."

Myrtle

When the sea broke through the Gap that night, Myrtle Beamish was sitting by the fire in the little back parlor behind the post office and general store, knitting a small blue bonnet for young Mrs. Thrower's infant son. She was not very good at knitting and every now and again she stopped and frowned at the pattern on her lap.

"How d'yer slip a stitch, Ma?" she asked.

Mrs. Beamish made a clicking sound of annoyance with her tongue. She was doing the post office accounts.

"Yew must wait a minute, Myrtle, till I've finished me sums."

But the minute stretched to ten. The cuckoo clock tapped out the seconds woodenly, filling the room with the noise of passing time. The cat, seeing his mistress sitting idle, jumped on the arm of Myrtle's chair and butted her cheek with his nose. He wanted her to tickle his fur.

"Dear Catty," she murmured, burying her face in his coat.

Then, the back door flew open, and in swept the flood. A great wall of water roared into the room.

"Ma!" shouted Myrtle.

"My lor!" exclaimed Mrs. Beamish.

The fire went out with a great steamy hiss, and the water swirled round the room as high as their knees.

"Open the door up the stairs," shouted Mrs. Beamish.

Myrtle grabbed the cat and opened the door but, before she could reach the bottom stair, a second wave broke into the room. Myrtle and Mrs. Beamish and the cat were struggling with the water up to their necks.

Myrtle freed herself from the clawing cat and flung him up the stairs.

"It's all right, Ma. It's all right," she said as she turned to help her mother.

Mrs. Beamish had been flung by the second wave against the sharp corner of the mantelshelf. Her head was streaming with blood.

"It'll be all right, Ma," said Myrtle, grasping her mother under the arms and struggling toward the stairs.

"Course it will, me gal," murmured Mrs. Beamish, as she tottered up to the room above, the blood streaming down on to her wet clothes.

"Course it will. Course it will," she kept repeating, after Myrtle had laid her on the bed, and was mopping the ugly cut.

Suddenly Mrs. Beamish sat upright.

"The post office!" she exclaimed.

"What about it?"

"I must go down and get the cash book and the postal orders."

Myrtle looked at her mother in astonishment.

"But yew can't, Ma. It's all under the water, and yew've hurt yer head."

"No," said Mrs. Beamish, struggling to her feet. "The post office'll only be up to me knees."

It was perfectly true. You climbed up four steps out of the parlor into the shop.

"Yew sit down there, Ma," ordered Myrtle, sticking out her chin. "I'll hev a try."

She looked out of the dormer window at the front and peered down into the street below. Ma was right. The water stood only two feet up the side of the post box.

"I'll go," said Myrtle, starting to squeeze herself out of the little window. "What else d'yer want?"

"The cash book, the postal orders, and the petty cash."

"What about the things in the shop?" she asked, grasping the reed thatch and feeling for the large nail in the wall with her foot.

"Them's ours, Myrtle. It's the Government stuff that's worritin' me."

Myrtle was clambering down the rough lath and plaster wall, helped by the creeper and the rusty nails, when Mrs. Beamish staggered to the window and called down after her.

"And the date stamp, Myrtle, don't forget the date stamp. That's the most important of all."

What a fool she was!

As she waded in the village street outside the shop, Myrtle remembered that she had forgotten to ask her mother for the key.

The top half of the shop door was made of glass. Dare she break it? Of course. But what with? The only thing near at hand was the ice-cream litter basket clamped to the shop wall. She wrenched it free and banged it with all her might at the glass of the door.

"Cor!" she thought to herself as she slid her arm through the jagged hole and turned up the yale lock. "Cor! This place ain't arf easy to burgle."

Inside the shop, she turned on the light and waded past the packing cases of oranges and the stand where her mother kept the poundcakes, till she came to the shelf of knitting wool. Behind a bale of double knit, on a little brass hook, hung the post office keys.

Suddenly she was in darkness. The electric lights had gone out all over the village.

Myrtle grasped the keys, climbed over the counter, and dropped down on the other side. Behind the wire cage she groped for the precious drawer where her mother kept the petty cash. Here was the cash book, too; she knew it by its shape; and these, with luck, were the postal orders. But how should she carry all these things?

Feeling her way with her hands along the wall, she came to the little lobby where Mr. Bell hung his postman's bag. Cash book, petty cash, postal orders, and date stamp—she threw all in the postman's bag and groped her way back through the shop.

"Might as well hev a few-sweets," she thought and threw a box of mint chocolates and a bundle of licorice sticks that stood high and dry on an upper shelf. "Might as well hev some enniseed balls, too," and she put her hand down into the aniseed jar.

By the time she had climbed back to the window, her eyes had become accustomed to the gloom.

"Got 'em all, Ma," she announced triumphantly, as she squeezed herself through.

But Mrs. Beamish made no reply.

"Ma!" exclaimed Myrtle. "Ma, where are yew?"

She found Mrs. Beamish lying on the bed, her eyes closed and her face gray and drawn with pain.

"Ma, what's the matter?"

Mrs. Beamish roused herself a little and opened her eyes. "I'm all right, me gal." She smiled weakly.

"I've got the things yew wanted," faltered Myrtle.

Looking at her mother lying there so ill and helpless and unlike herself, she felt her lips begin to wobble. She was sure she was going to cry.

"I'll get yew out of yer wet clothes," she gulped. "It's awful cold tonight."

Myrtle took off her mother's wet clothes and rubbed her with a blanket; and then she helped her into fresh underclothes and her thickest jumper and skirt.

"Yer a good gal," smiled her mother.

But she still looked very ill and she trembled all over.

"Yew must put on yer coat, Ma," said Myrtle, slipping her mother's right arm into the sleeve.

Then she got out of her own wet clothes, and dried herself with another blanket, and dressed herself in the warmest things she could find. And then she rubbed down the poor, wet cat.

Suddenly another great wave shook the cottage. Water slapped up the stairs into the bedroom.

"We'll hev to git out on the roof, Ma," cried Myrtle.

They climbed out of the back bedroom window—the one that overlooked the Broad—for out at the back the roof of the coal shed gave them a step up onto the roof. All the same, it was a great effort for them and, by the time Myrtle had heaved her mother and the cat and herself up on to the thatch, they were all exhausted.

Down below, the water crept higher and higher up the walls of the cottage. Up on the roof, they lay with their faces close to the reeds, feeling the wind sweeping over their backs and the cold spatter of rain landing on their hands and cheeks. They clutched at the thatch with their numbed fingers and braced their feet against the upraised pattern of rushes that the thatcher had made along the edge of the eaves. The cat seemed very unhappy. He stuck his claws into the shoulder of Myrtle's coat and miaowed loudly in her face.

Myrtle looked anxiously at her mother lying beside her.

"She must've hurt herself real bad on that mantelshelf," she thought.

It was unlike her mother to be so silent and meek. She did not know quite what she expected her to say, as they lay stretched out there in the teeth of the wind; but her daughter knew that if she had been herself, Mrs. Beamish would have had plenty to say.

Gaining a little confidence and sensing that her mother was safe where she was, Myrtle unhooked the cat from her coat and gently pulled herself up the slope of the roof. When she came to the top, she put one leg over the axle beam, and sat astride the cottage and peered north through the darkness up Reedsmere Street.

On the roof next door she could see dim figures perched across the ridge pole, just like herself. She could hear them shouting to each other and to the people across the street. Five houses away, someone had a flashlight and was waving it backward and forward, as though signaling a message. In a lull in the storm, she thought she heard the splash of oars.

"Hi, there," yelled Myrtle, "come and help us. Ma's hurt her head."

But the northwest gale blew the words back in her face, and out across the River Thirl and away down the coast to the south. She tried again. No one on the roofs up the street heard her cries or turned to see her waving on top of the cottage thatch.

Reedsmere Post Office stood by itself—fifty yards from the Thurgar's house next door—the very last cottage in the street. It was built right down on the wharf, where the houseboats and the yachts moored in summertime before setting back down the Thirl toward Wroxham. It was the very worst place in the world for a cottage to stand, on the night of that terrible gale.

The sea race, which Mark and Mary had crossed with such peril in the middle of the Broad, when it reached Reedsmere Village became caught in the turning tide of the Thirl. It swooped into the river as into a funnel, cutting away the wharf and beating against the cottage that stood on the quay side. Myrtle could see the lips of the salt water frothing like

an angry beast at the walls of her home. As she looked down
the river, she saw hen coops and crates and spars and oars
tossing inland on top of the crested waves.

Suddenly, while she sat on the ridge of the roof, the
cottage shuddered and groaned in the grip of the flood.

She slid quickly back down the slope of the roof.

"Come on, Ma," she said. "We'd best sit on the coal-house
roof."

"Why?" murmured the dazed Mrs. Beamish.

"Cos the house is goin' to fall down. That's why."

Myrtle put the cat inside the postman's bag and then very
gently pushed and pulled her mother back the way they had
come.

It was a tiny roof, and the water surged only a foot below
the tiles; but it was almost flat, and the building below stood
as firm as a rock. All the coal houses in Reedsmere were old
air-raid shelters that the Council had put up in 1939.

Hardly a minute had passed before Myrtle, who was
watching the line of the thatch against the raging sky, saw
the whole building slowly sink into the flood. It was silent
and unbearable, like the death of a ship. The walls had
crumbled away; the dormer window had disappeared; and
now, the reeds of the thatch were swirling down the river
Thirl.

Myrtle sat with her mother's head in her lap, tears streaming down her cheeks.

It had been such a happy home for them both.

Reedsmere Hall

Though more than a hundred people had found their way through the flood to the Hall, Dr. and Mrs. Vaughan were not there. Hepzie and Mary learned this immediately at the entrance to the Rest Center.

Miss Yoxford, her father's secretary, was standing by the door to the Long Room with a large drawing board, upon which were pinned house-to-house lists of the inhabitants of Reedsmere.

"Mary, I'm so glad to see you," she said. "And you too, Mrs. Foulger. Thank goodness we can tick your two names off. Where are Dr. and Mrs. Vaughan? Nurse Hitchcock has been asking for them both all evening."

"They're in Norwich," replied Mary dully.

"Address?"

Mary blinked.

"If we know the address, Mary, we can get the police to call them. The telephones are cut, but they've got walkie-talkies."

"They're with Dr. Paget. He lives in the Close."

"Fine." Miss Yoxford made a note, and then picked up her lists again. She was appallingly efficient. "And now what about Mark and Mr. Foulger?"

"We don't know, miss," put in Hepzie. "We're that worried. They went off in the doctor's rowboat, and . . ."

"Mark Vaughan . . . question mark. James Foulger . . . question mark. Well, don't worry. Go in now and get some hot cocoa from Mrs. Lardner."

Hepzie pressed Mary's hand.

"Never yew fret, luv," she murmured. "They're that moithered, they're all in a mix."

As soon as Hepzie and Mary entered the Long Room they saw how great the disaster was that had befallen their village.

The great room was full of shocked and bewildered people. The flood had swept as quickly and silently along Reedsmere Street as it had swept over the Vaughans' garden. It had caught whole families sitting around their firesides; worse still it had separated others.

"She only went out to see her sister just for an hour," old Mr. Clatworthy was saying. "Just for an hour, Mrs. Lardner, and she he'nt come home."

Lit only by candles and the fitful gleams from a great wood fire, the room was full not only of people but of the shadows of people, which stalked across the walls and stretched along the ceiling, and seemed to add to the restless confusion of the scene. Sudden spurts of firelight lit up familiar faces that Mary and Hepzie had known all their lives. Middle-aged Mrs. Poyser had been caught without her false teeth. In the firelight she looked like a face from a Rembrandt picture—as old as the hills. Miss Owles was sitting beside her wrapped in a scarlet blanket. And next to her, exhausted but at peace, sat young Mrs. Thrower, her newborn son in her arms.

Members of the Women's Voluntary Service had put up the two dozen army camp beds which belonged to the Rest Center and had turned the platform and the far end of the room into a kind of hospital. Into the beds they had put the very young and the very old. Mary saw the three carrotyheaded little Peachey girls sitting up in one bed, surveying the room with solemn sleepy eyes. Nothing seemed to surprise them. In the bed next door two babies were fast asleep. And beyond that the district nurse was attending to an old woman whose white hair tumbled down over the pillow.

"Ev yer seen my Maisie, miss?" Mr. Clatworthy asked Mary. "She only went out to see her sister just for an hour. Just for an hour, miss, that's all."

Mary shook her head. A great lump was rising in her throat.

"Oh, why aren't Father and Mother and Canon Crowfoot here?" she sobbed silently to herself. "Look how we all need them!"

No wonder Reedsmere was "moithered," and in "a mix."

Yet over by the fire to which she and Hepzie were pushing their way, people were laughing. The relief of being safe seemed to make them almost tipsy.

"And there she were," said Fred Aldis, "up in that little ole bedroom of hers, sayin', 'Yew always were one for a joke, Fred Aldis, but I h'en't goin' out in that crazy rowboat o' yours if it's the last thing I don't do.' Dan an me 'ad to pick her up and carry her down by force, we did."

Mary smiled in spite of herself.

"It sounds like Mrs. Dashwood," she thought.

And now they were welcoming them both to the circle around the fire. Ned Brewster slipped out of a chair and offered it to Hepzie.

"Well, Mrs. Foulger," grinned the toothless Mrs. Poyser. "Not much left of your cottage down by the Gap, I reckon."

"Not much," replied Hepzie, sharp and firm, as she sometimes was with people she did not like. "Not much 'cept the bedroom and the thatch, Mrs. Poyser."

Mary whispered to Ned.

"Where did they go, Ned, after they left you and Sandy?"

"Why, back to the church to pick you all up."

Mary shook her head, but said nothing. It was too weary and hopeless a task to tell him about *Donovan* floating empty down the Broad.

And now Mrs. Lardner had come up to her, carrying a tray laden with cups of cocoa.

"Take one, my dear. It'll put the color back into your cheeks."

Mary shook her head again.

"Come along, you try, Mary. We've all got to try tonight."

"You leave her be, Mrs. Lardner," interrupted Hepzie. "Miss Mary never were a one for hot cocoa. It makes her sick."

Mary looked around desperately for Myrtle's bright mop of hair. If only Myrtle were here, she would somehow feel braver and less alone. But there was no Myrtle, and no Mrs. Beamish. Where *could* they be?

Sick at heart, she found her way to one particular window seat, hidden in the shadows, far away from the fire. It had a sweet, musty smell, which came from the toy cupboard underneath. She knew all about the toy cupboard and the smell. Mark and she had once found a little Indian brass censer there with a black pyramid of incense inside, during one of those long, trying afternoons when they had been asked up to the Hall to play with Gervaise and Geraint Speke. Mark had lit the incense and set it aglow and swung the censer around the room, pretending he was an Indian priest.

Mark! Every thought of him made her ache with pain.

She clasped her knees very hard in her hands and tried to make herself think of what was passing in front of her eyes.

As in a dream, she saw Sir Bartlett enter the Long Room carrying a pile of pink and pale blue blankets. They looked thick and fleecy, quite unlike the gray, coarse, scratchy blankets that had been issued to the Rest Center. Lady Speke followed, carrying sheets and pillow cases. Both were in evening dress, Sir Bartlett in a dinner jacket and his wife in a rustling short taffeta dress that glinted richly in the warm candlelight.

"They both look so kind and nice," thought Mary. "I wonder why they have such awful children?"

Lady Speke and Nurse Hitchcock were making up a proper bed for the old woman whose hair had tumbled down. They moved with the precision of experts.

"Very odd!" thought Mary. "You'd never think anyone so elegant could be so practical."

Sir Bartlett had sat down beside Mr. Clatworthy, and in a man's way, Mary supposed, was trying to comfort him.

Slowly the room was filling up. Four more choirboys had arrived by now, their faces stung by the cold and their hair powdered with snow. They took off their wet coats and crept in by the fire, lying as flat as they could on the floor so that the people behind them could still see the flames. Mrs. Lardner was busy with her cocoa cups. The three little Peachey girls had fallen asleep in three crumpled little heaps. People crossed and recrossed the Long Room, their weird, elongated shadows moving darkly across the Gainsborough portraits.

Outside, the wind still roared in the elms and sent gusts of sleet snapping against the window panes behind her. There was no avoiding the gale. It blew into every cranny of one's brain.

Quite suddenly, Mary found that Canon Crowfoot was standing beside her.

"Take an old man's advice, Mary," he said, smiling sadly. "At times like this it's best to be doing something. Mrs. Lardner wants help in washing up those cocoa cups."

Mary blushed and got to her feet.

"How stupid of me," she said. "I'm so sorry. Of course, I should be helping."

"I was not reproving you, my dear. It's just how things are. You wash the cups. I'll sit with Mr. Clatworthy."

The canteen was full of chattering, hurrying women—filling hot-water bottles, hanging wet clothes round the gas fire, mixing dry milk, washing up.

"May I help?"

A silence fell for a moment.

"Of course you can," said Miss Cotterel kindly. "Take this tray, Mary, and fetch the cups from those boys lying round the fire next door."

Then followed what seemed an endless time of washing off the wrinkled bits of cocoa skin and drying the cups with a dish towel that was far too wet; while all about her the women bustled and talked.

"It's Amy Beamish we want here tonight," said one. "She always were a one at a time like this!"

What *had* happened to Myrtle and Mrs. Beamish? Why weren't they here?

At last there seemed to be no more cups to dry and no more wet clothes to arrange on the airers. The choirboys were asleep. Ben Blaza and the crowd from the Pickerel Inn were sitting on chairs in the gallery. Except for Mark and Jim and Mrs. Clatworthy and Myrtle and her mother and old Dotty Dick, all the inhabitants of Reedsmere were known to be safe. Dr. and Mrs. Vaughan were either in Norwich or on their way home, and young Billy Lane and his fiancée had gone to the city too, to see *Dick Whittington* at the Royal Theatre. Nothing could happen to them. The flood stopped at the lodge gates.

All safe except six! It seemed a miracle.

Mary was back in her window seat when Dotty Dick

tottered in. He was supported by Miss Yoxford, who beckoned Canon Crowfoot over to them.

"Well, Mr. Dack," smiled the Vicar. "We're delighted you're safe. Where have you been?"

The District Nurse clucked her teeth.

"Off with those wet clothes. Quick everyone. Space by the fire."

Mrs. Lardner appeared with a hot-water bottle and Miss Cotterel with a fleecy pink blanket.

"Where ever hev you bin, Dick Dack?" asked the toothless Mrs. Poyser.

But Dotty Dick just shook his head and grinned and mumbled. He had never been able to speak so that anyone could understand him.

"That young American landed him at the lodge three minutes ago," explained Miss Yoxford. "The boy was off again so quick they didn't have time to ask him where he had found him."

"That boy's a bin in that cold water up to his waist for over two hours!" exclaimed Hepzie, her eyes bright.

"He's a brave lad, and no mistake," said the mother of one of the choirboys.

Dotty Dick was sitting naked now, wrapped only in the Spekes' pink blanket, his feet in a basin of hot water and a hot-water bottle on his lap. His face was regaining a little of its color.

"Hev yer seen me Jim, Dick?" asked Hepzie.

"Or Mrs. Clatworthy?" asked Ben Blaza, who had come down from the gallery.

"Or the Vaughan boy?" asked Mrs. Poyser.

"Or Mrs. Beamish and her girl?" asked Miss Owles.

But it was useless. Dotty Dick just grinned and muttered as he had grinned and muttered for nearly seventy years. No one could get any sense out of him.

The sight of Dick brought Mary up sharply against her

grief. Was it really only this afternoon that Father had thought of punishing Mark for breaking his windows? She had lived through a lifetime since then.

And then suddenly, there was Mark! There was Jim! They stood in the doorway blinking at the light.

"Hey, Nurse Hitchcock," bawled Jim. "Yew best run down quick to the lodge. That American boy's fainted with the cold."

"Bring bottles and blankets," said the nurse quickly to Mrs. Lardner, "and the brandy too. There's some at the back of the Red Cross Cupboard."

Hepzie's face was streaming with tears. Jim, soaked to the skin, stood comforting her, with the water dropping off in puddles round her chair.

"There, Mother. There, Mother," was all he could say.

And Mark? A strange, strained, anguished Mark ran across the room and buried his head in Mary's lap.

"Oh, Mark," whispered Mary. "I thought I'd never see you again." And her tears dropped plop onto Mark's wet hair. "What happened? Why did you leave *Donovan?*"

She hugged him fiercely in her arms, and Mark buried himself even deeper in her lap.

All eyes were on either Jim or Mark.

"Me and the boy went to save Dick," boomed Jim. "And a fine time we had of it. Got marooned on that rotten old thatch of his."

"What happened to your boat?" asked the Canon.

"Oh, it sort of slipped away, it did," replied Jim.

Mark got to his feet, his face crimson.

"No, it didn't," he cried. "I tied the beastly knot all wrong. I never can tie a clove hitch."

In the silence that followed, Mark turned back to Mary, sick with shame.

"You'd no call to tell them that, boy," said Jim quietly.

But before anyone had time to digest this remark the whole room shook with laughter, a huge, gusty, rollicking laughter that surged in a great wave up over the gallery railing to the roof—a laughter born of relief from their intolerable tension. Three more were safe.

Yet three were still missing. The laughter died on their lips, as the people of Reedsmere turned their eyes toward the desolate Mr. Clatworthy, and remembered jolly Mrs. Beamish and Myrtle.

Mark's face was torn with misery. Mary folded him in her arms.

"They're not laughing at you, Mark," she whispered.

"They're laughing because you and Jim are safe. We've all been so worried. Oh, Mark, smile. It's all over. The nightmare is over. You're safe."

It was then that Mary realized how wet he was. Miss Cotterel was beside them with a towel and a blue blanket.

"Quick, Mark. Off with your clothes." She smiled. "Rub yourself hard with this. It's a new scratchy towel. You'll soon get yourself warm. Mary'll help you and get you something hot to drink."

Twenty minutes later Mark was fast asleep. He had collapsed in a blue blanket heap as humpy as those of the three little Peachey girls. Mary, squashed by his largeness into far too small a corner, watched over the heap as it moved rhythmically up and down to his long, deep breathing.

And then she closed her eyes.

"It's only Myrtle and Mrs. Beamish and Mrs. Clatworthy now," she prayed. "Oh, please, please, let them be safe too."

In the Middle of the Night

Mrs. Vaughan arrived at the Rest Center at a quarter to twelve. She looked anxiously across the drowsy room, over people nodding uncomfortably in chairs, over Rest Center beds full of babies and old people, past a group of white-aproned women whispering softly in a little group, till her eyes fell on the window seat where Mark and Mary lay.

How white and tired Mary looked! And what an odd lump Mark made under the Spekes' blue blanket! She could see his naked heel and instep sticking out one end. How relieved she was to see that white face and that boot-stained foot! It had been a nightmare, since she and John had received the police call in Norwich an hour ago.

As she stood by the window seat, Mary opened her eyes.

"Mary, darling," Mrs. Vaughan murmured as she stooped to kiss her.

Mary put her arms around her mother's neck and buried her face in the collar of her soft fur coat, just as she had done six hours earlier that evening, when she had hugged her mother good-bye at home.

"Don't wake Mark," she whispered. "He's had a terrible night."

Then, slipping her knees out very gently from under Mark's head, she got to her feet and stood by her mother.

"Where's Father?" she asked.

Her mother took her hand in hers.

"He's gone out with Mr. Farrow in Tom Wright's row-boat."

"Where?"

"Mary, you've got to be very brave."

"What's happened?"

"The post office has been washed away."

"Oh, Mother! Myrtle and Mrs. Beamish!"

Mrs. Vaughan nodded her head.

"And Father's gone out to look for them?"

"Of course."

Mary looked up into her mother's face.

"Of course he has," she said calmly.

Mrs. Lardner was tiptoeing toward them.

"So glad to see you, Mrs. Vaughan," she whispered hoarsely. "We've got a pot of tea and a battery wireless in the canteen. We thought we'd listen to the midnight news. Would you care to join us?"

So once again that night Mary and her mother stood by a wireless listening for the latest news of the great gale. They stood in a circle—Ben Blaza and his friends from the Pickerel Inn, Mrs. Lardner and her band of helpers, Mary, her mother, and Miss Yoxford.

Out of the cracklings and sighings of the storm the announcer's voice suddenly dropped, round and clear.

"The British Railways Motor Vessel *Princess Victoria* foundered at three o'clock this afternoon in a severe gale off the Irish coast. There were 177 people on board. There is news so far of between forty and fifty survivors."

"How terrible!" gasped Miss Yoxford.

"Fifteen miles east of Withernsea, in Yorkshire," continued the announcer, "a motor vessel has broken away from its tow and is drifting with a skeleton crew on board. Communications with the lifeboat at Spurn Point have broken down. The lifeboat authorities ask that any person hearing this who is in the neighborhood of Spurn Point should contact the Coastguard at Spurn or the lifeboat station . . . There is a warning from the police of a possibility of an exceptionally high tide in the rivers Thames and Medway. High water at London Bridge is one minute past three A.M."

Ben Blaza let out a savage laugh.

"An hexceptional 'igh tide at Reedsmere in Norfolk, what drownded a 'ole village out of their 'omes don't interest the nobs in London, I reckon!"

"But communications have all broken down, Mr. Blaza," said Mrs. Lardner severely. "You heard that, didn't you?"

"All the telephone wires are down for miles around," put in Miss Yoxford.

"No one knows yet what things are like here," explained Mrs. Vaughan.

"I reckon the whole east coast has bust open," growled Dan Ball gloomily, "from Withernsea right down to Harwich."

Mary turned to her mother in bewilderment.

"But I don't understand," she said. "Has this awful flood not really reached the Thames yet?"

"No, Mary. High tide comes to the coast towns later the further south you go. I believe there's four, or is it five hours' difference between the time of high water at King's Lynn and at Great Yarmouth."

Mary saw, in her mind's eye, a huge tidal wave moving slowly and relentlessly down the North Sea, like some gigantic prehistoric monster risen from the depths of the ocean.

"And it'll go crash against the Dutch sand dunes at about breakfast time tomorrow," she thought.

"Oh, Mother, poor Holland! Poor us! Poor everybody!" she gasped aloud.

At half-past twelve, a message came in from the American

air base that Mrs. Clatworthy was safe. She had gone to visit her sister in the hamlet of Thirlsted, a mile down the river. Caught by the flood in her sister's bungalow, they had both been rescued by the Americans in the nick of time.

"I couldn't believe my Maisie had left me, somehow," old Mr. Clatworthy confided to Canon Crowfoot. "She'd a told me she were dead, she would. I've been lying here, waiting for her voice. But she h'en't said a word all night."

Mary and her mother sat together in a window seat near the door, waiting for Dr. Vaughan to return. Both of them, sick at heart, were imagining the worst that might have happened at the end of Reedsmere Street. They saw the post office washed away with Mrs. Beamish and Myrtle trapped inside.

Kitty Vaughan shuddered. It was too horrible. She had known Amy Beamish all her married life. Their daughters had been born the same summer just before the war, and they had struggled together through all the anxious years while their husbands were abroad—through air raids and rationing and the terrible coal-less winter after the war—and they had come to respect and treasure each other as only good neighbors can.

"Poor Amy. Poor Amy," said Mrs. Vaughan, over and over again to herself. "To have come through so much and to end like this!"

But Mary could not believe that Myrtle was dead. Myrtle was far too vivid and alive to die.

"She'll find a way out. I know she will," she thought, as she twisted and twisted the frayed wool on the cuff of her jumper sleeve.

She was right. Myrtle could not be dead. She was standing there in the doorway, looking as though she had drowned and come to life again.

"Myrtle!" shouted Mary, running toward her.

Myrtle's hair was plastered wet against her cheeks, and her wet clothes clung to her legs.

"Myrtle!"

But Myrtle did not seem to hear or see. She stood white-faced and frowning and dazed.

"It's me—Mary. What's happened?"

Before Myrtle could come to herself and speak, Mary saw Dr. Vaughan towering behind her. He was carrying Mrs. Beamish in his arms.

Mrs. Beamish looked as though she had drowned and not come to life again. Her eyes were shut, and the cut on her forehead stood out livid and angry against the pallor of her cheeks.

"Mary, go and get your mother quickly," her father said. But Mrs. Vaughan was already beside him.

"Dead?" she whispered.

Dr. Vaughan shook his head.

"No," he said.

Very slowly, very gently, they carried the injured woman down the darkened room toward the fire.

"It's Amy," whispered one of the white-aproned women. "It's Amy Beamish."

When she saw with what love they took off her mother's soaking clothes, and rubbed her, and warmed her, and laid her in a bed, Myrtle's long-enduring self-control gave way. She flung her arms round Mary and noiselessly sobbed and sobbed. Mary could feel the warm tears trickling down her neck.

"Oh, Myrtle, she'll be all right now. I know she will," whispered Mary.

And then she became aware of the coldness of Myrtle's cheek and the wetness of her embrace.

"Quick. Take all your clothes off. I'll get you a towel and a blanket."

Two minutes later Myrtle sat shivering in a fleecy blue

blanket, with her wet clothes and the postman's bag on the floor in front of her.

"What've you got there?" asked Mary, for the postman's bag was heaving up and down like a living thing.

"Catty."

"What, your Catty?"

Myrtle nodded her head and smiled faintly. Her teeth were chattering so much that she could hardly speak.

Mary stooped down and pulled out the wettest and most crestfallen cat she had ever seen. It gave a huge miaow and ran off into the shadows before Mary could grab a towel to rub it dry.

"Come to the fire, Myrtle," said Miss Cotterel gently. "We'll have you warm and feeling better in no time, won't we, Mary?"

Up on the platform, the white-aproned women were gliding to and fro with pillows and hot-water bottles and cups of tea. Dr. Vaughan and his wife knelt one on each side of Mrs. Beamish's bed, gently massaging her arms and chest. No one seemed to notice that the doctor in his evening clothes was quite as wet as the Beamishes had been.

When Mary returned with hot milk to the fireside, she found the cat curled up in Myrtle's lap.

"Here you are. Here's something hot," she said.

Myrtle smiled. She put her finger into the hot milk and put a blob of it on the tip of the cat's nose.

Mary smiled too.

Myrtle was going to be all right again. This was the Myrtle she had always known.

Two hours later, Mary stirred restlessly on the floor by the fire. She was dreaming of *Donovan* floating down the Broad. Then she woke up and opened her eyes.

Myrtle was fast asleep, with her head resting in the crook of Mary's knees. The firelight flickered over her face, catching the gleams in her bright hair and deepening the hollows around her eyes. Mary had never seen anyone look so exhausted.

"She looks as though she could sleep for a week," she thought.

Then, propping her head up on one hand, Mary gazed around the room. She could not see her father or mother. They had gone from the platform, and Canon Crowfoot had taken their place. He was sitting beside Mrs. Beamish, reading a little black book. Was Mrs. Beamish dead? Just at that moment she must have stirred, for Canon Crowfoot laid down his book and moved her pillow to one side. Mary sighed with relief.

She looked around sleepily at the worn-out inhabitants of Reedsmere Village. Mrs. Poyser was asleep with her mouth wide open. Hepzie sat with her head nodding forward over her chest. Jim, Ned, Mark, Sandy Catchpole, Jimmy Bell—they were all there in the shadows—all safe, all well.

And here in the warm glow of the fire, curled up in the crook of her knees, lay Myrtle and Myrtle's cat.

Candlemas Eve

Soon after six o'clock in the morning, the whole room was stirring. People stretched aching shoulders and cramped limbs; the babies started whimpering for their early morning feeding, and one of Mrs. Lardner's helpers dropped a pile of saucers in the canteen next door.

Mary opened her eyes to the unaccustomed glare. The electricity supply had been restored. Its harsh whiteness revealed what the warm firelight had kept hidden. She saw that Jim and Hepzie looked old and ill, that the hollows of Mrs. Poyser's eyes were black, and that young Mrs. Thrower was almost fainting with fatigue. Everyone looked creased and crumpled and faintly gray.

During the night someone had lifted the sleeping Myrtle from Mary's knees and put her in a bed beside her mother. Mary found her fast asleep with her cat stretched out on her chest.

"Don't wake her," whispered Mrs. Vaughan. "We want her to sleep as long as she can."

"How's Mrs. Beamish?"

"Still unconscious, but no worse. As soon as Father can get an ambulance he's sending her into the Norfolk and Norwich Hospital."

"Is she as bad as that?"

"With a head injury it's never wise to take a risk."

Mark started heaving under the blue blanket, and slowly poked out a round, sleepy face.

"Fetch his clothes from the canteen, Mary," her mother said. "They're quite dry. When he's dressed, I want you both to go down to the Hall Farm and fetch whatever eggs Mr. Smith can let you have. Take Ned and Jimmy Bell and Sandy too. They might be able to help with the milk."

As they all ran down the lane in the gray dawn with the great wind still threshing in the elm trees, sending twigs and bits of straw flying across the air, Mary peered critically at her brother.

"You look awful," she muttered sideways, so that the others could not hear.

"Why?"

"So dirty."

"Can't help that. You don't look so good yourself."

When they reached the farm all the lights were blazing in the battery house and the cowsheds and the farm kitchen. It looked like a little city lit up at night.

Mrs. Smith was waiting for them in the kitchen with three buckets of eggs.

The boys surged around her, all eager to be the first to tell her of the night's extraordinary events.

"The water come right up the church, Mrs. Smith," said Sandy.

"The post office's been washed away!" exclaimed Ned.

"And, Mrs. Beamish," added Jimmy Bell. "She's got a great bash on her 'ed."

"And Mr. Clatworthy," added Sandy, not to be outdone. "He's lost Mrs. Clatworthy. But he's got his ole canary."

The rest of the Smith family came tumbling out of bed to hear the news, and stood in a ring around the boys, hanging on their words as though they were shipwrecked mariners.

"Lost Mrs. Clatworthy?" asked Mrs. Smith anxiously.

"No, she's all right," put in Mary. "News came through

when you were all asleep. The Americans rescued her. She's
at their base."

"And a Yank like a spaceman came and rescued us all in
his rubber boat," shouted Jimmy Bell.

"A Yank like a spaceman?" asked the younger Smiths in
chorus.

But Mrs. Smith was not attending. She was asking Mary
about Mrs. Beamish.

"Mother says she's to be taken into hospital as soon as
Father can get hold of an ambulance," Mary told her.

Just then, Mr. Smith appeared, trundling a small churn of
milk over the cobbles outside the kitchen door.

"That's not enough, Joe," said Mrs. Smith. "Not for all that
lot. How many are there of you up at the Hall, do you think,
Mary?"

"About a hundred."

"No," contradicted Mark. "A hundred and fifty."

"Garn!" said Ned. "There's 'bout three hundred, at least."

"Aren't that number of people in Reedsmere, Ned," smiled
Mrs. Smith. "Go and get the big churn, Joe. Reedsmere come
afore the Norfolk Creameries at a time like this."

"And I'll bring the truck round to take you all back,"
shouted Mr. Smith over his shoulder, as he hurried into the
gloaming.

Mrs. Smith surveyed the tired, dirty young faces in front of
her.

"Tell you what," she said. "I've got a great tub of hot water
out in the scullery. Would you like a wash and a tidy up?"

The boys did not think that they would like either the one
or the other. But Mary tugged at Mark.

"Come along," she said.

Mark looked so pleased with himself, paddling in the hot
water, that gradually all the others followed suit. They found
it wonderful to have their feet warm again; it made them feel
quite different.

"How did you know Mr. Clatworthy had saved his canary?" Mary asked Sandy as she tugged a comb through his hair.

"He had his ole cage down alongside his ole bed, that's why," replied Sandy.

"I didn't see it."

"It were all covered up with his ole coat. Canary birds don't like a lot o' racket at night. They allus cover them up, they do."

When they drove up to Reedsmere Hall, they found an ambulance waiting at the door leading into the Long Room. Myrtle, now fully dressed in her dried clothes, was wearing her stubborn look.

"I'm goin' with Ma," she said fiercely to Mrs. Lardner.

"But Myrtle, you'd much better stay here with us. You can't do anything for your mother in hospital."

"I'm goin' with me Ma," Myrtle repeated, sticking out her chin.

Mary jumped out of the truck and ran to her friend.

"What's all this?" asked Dr. Vaughan, as he came out of the Long Room door.

"Myrtle's being silly," said Mrs. Lardner. "She insists upon going into Norwich with her mother."

"Very right and proper too," said Dr. Vaughan.

Mrs. Vaughan slipped her arm under Myrtle's.

"I'd like to come too, if I may. Then when we've seen your mother safely into bed, we'll wait a little to hear what the doctor says, and then we'll come home."

Mary gave Myrtle a hug.

"Oh, Myrtle, it'll be such fun! We'll make up a bed in my room. Would you like that?"

Myrtle gave Mary a tired smile and handed her the cat.

"I'll take care of Catty," said Mary. "He'll be waiting for you at home when you come back."

Back in the Long Room, a space had been cleared and three trestle tables had been erected, upon which Sir Bartlett Speke was slowly piling the contents of his wife's storage cupboard as he brought them out in hamper loads. There were cartons of Corn Flakes and Rice Crispies, pots of marmalade and jam, tins of sardines, and packets of sugar and tea and biscuits.

"Looks like a stall at the Church Bazaar," whispered Mary to Mark.

When breakfast was over and the Rest Center tidied, Canon Crowfoot stood on the platform and addressed his parishioners.

"Last night," he said, "our village suffered a great disaster. Yet not one of us has lost his life. All our nearest and dearest stand safe beside us. Today is Candlemas Eve. Let us go to our church this morning with full hearts to give thanks to God for our deliverance.

"The flood has gone down several feet and, at Hollow Bridge, there's only a twenty-yard stretch of water across the road. Those of you who have rubber boots can carry the smaller children on your backs. On the raised footpath the water can't be more than six inches deep. The rest of us can be rowed across in the Pickerel boats, but Mr. Blaza will want help from you younger and stronger men to carry them from the lodge gates down to the water's edge."

"Blimey, they look a rum lot!" whispered Ned Brewster to Jimmy Bell as they peered through the vestry curtains at the people of Reedsmere filing into their pews in church.

Hepzie, still clad in her flowered eiderdown, was being pushed up the aisle in an old bath chair by Dr. Vaughan clad in Sir Bartlett's last year's tweeds. Behind them walked Mrs. Poyser and Miss Owles, still clinging to their blankets, while in their wake shambled Dotty Dick, all creased and crumbled in his poor shrunk clothes.

"Cor! He's brought his canary with him!" exclaimed Jimmy.

"Who? Where?"

"Old Mr. Clatworthy. Over there by the door."

"Bet it'll start singin' in the wrong place," whispered Ned. "Hope it does."

"And there's Mary Vaughan with Myrtle's cat!"

Mary walked beside Mark, holding Catty in her arms. The cat clung to the front of her jumper and pulled at the threads.

The cold in the church was numbing. No one knelt, because the hassocks were like wet sponges. When Miss Cotterel pulled out the organ stops and began to play, Canon Crowfoot and the choir walked up the aisle in their over-coats. Their surplices, left hanging in the vestry all night, had trailed in the flood and were dripping with water.

"Down with the rosemary and bays,"

sang the boys,

"Down with the mistletoe;
Instead of holly, now upraise
The greener box, for show."

The Candlemas service had begun.

The people of Reedsmere, in their strange attire, listened to the beautiful Candlemas collect and to Canon Crowfoot reading the gospel of the Visit to the Temple, with a new awareness of its message to them all. And then, old and young—Mr. Clatworthy, Hepzie, Dr. Vaughan, Mary, Mark, and the three little Peachey girls—all joined in singing Simeon's song.

Mary gazed up the chancel and thought of the horror of last night. There on the altar, to remind her of it all, lay Mark's rugger ball and her violin, where she had placed them, safe above the flood.

Canon Crowfoot had thrown away the sermon he had written in his garden on Thursday morning. He stood, not in the pulpit, but on the chancel step, and as he spoke he looked at his parishioners one by one, as though he were talking to them in their own homes.

"You have borne yourselves bravely in a night that has tested us all," he said. "But today and tomorrow and the next day are going to test us even more. We shall return from the service to sodden homes and flooded fields and gardens. Mrs. Beamish and Myrtle have no home at all. All of us need courage, and all of us must show kindness and Christian neighborliness to one another.

"Every one of us, however old or however young, has a clear duty to perform.

"As soon as we have taken our families home, every man of us must take ourselves with spades and shovels to Reedsmere Gap. The police tell me that trucks of sandbags are on the way. We must close that Gap before the next spring tide. You know what will happen to our village if we fail in this.

"You women have, perhaps, the hardest task of all. Your homes are the centers of your lives; you will find them dirtied with wet mud and sand, perhaps even still flooded. You must do what you can till we can help you clean them. If conditions are such that you cannot feed and warm your families in your own homes, then you must stay at the Rest Center. Remember always that people are more important than goods and chattels. Cling to the knowledge that your husbands and children are safe, and don't grieve too much for the best linoleum. Make a home, a smiling home for your families, even if it is in the bedroom upstairs or in a small corner of the Long Room."

Next Canon Crowfoot looked at Mary and Mark and then turned to his choirboys.

"You young people have a duty, too. Help us all with your cheerfulness. Meals will be late, homes will be cold, cherished possessions will be lost. Remember that these things are worse for the old to bear than they are for you who are young. Help us with your hands and with your laughter to get the world back to its tidy routine again.

"And you younger ones," he continued, smiling at the little Peachey girls. "You can help too. When you feel cold and hungry, don't cry. See what little thing you can do to help your fathers and mothers. Think of them. Remember that they are going to be too busy to give you all the time that you have been used to expect from them. See if you cannot help to mother those even younger than yourselves. Be obedient, and keep a smile ready for us old people. We shall need those smiles.

"Now let us sing that beautiful hymn we all love, written by the poet William Cowper in another 'time of trouble.' Number 373 in your Hymn Books."

> "God moves in a mysterious way
>   His wonders to perform
> He plants his footsteps in the sea,
>   And rides upon the storm."

Home Again

The snow was blowing level across the ground as the Vaughans drove out of the gates of the south lodge on the upper road.

"The lower road will be impassable," said Dr. Vaughan, as he took the turning inland.

"Do you mean we've got to go all around by Thirlsthwaite to get home?" asked Mark, trying to stop himself from shivering.

"Yes. The Thirl has broken its banks on either side of the bridge on the lower road. We'll have to cross by the big bridge on the Norwich road."

"So each time we want to go to the village, we've got to go three miles round?"

They had reached the highest point in the upper road and Dr. Vaughan, having found a gap in the hedge by a gate, stopped the car.

"I don't think that you'll want to be going to the village much till the floods go down," he observed. "Look."

Below them, along the edge of the water meadows, straggled the houses of Reedsmere Street. They looked forlorn, pathetic—like old toys forgotten and no longer loved. Two policemen—they looked like Constables Bent and Cattermole from Thirlsthwaite—were rowing down the street in a small dinghy. A man in a duck punt floated over the place where the post office had once stood.

Mary stared at it silently, feeling a lump rising in her throat.

Silently they gazed at the ruined countryside they knew so well. Beyond the village stretched the Broad, now three times its normal size, and beyond that, separated only by the thin line of the top of the Marram Hills, rolled the gray North Sea. It was all horribly depressing. Near to the village, on the surface of the water, bobbed bits of hen coops, broken fences, bales of straw torn from a haystack, and in one place not far from the boundary of the Catchpoles' field, a large reddish-brown object floated inertly on the flood.

Mary turned her gaze inward and downward to Myrtle's cat, nestling on her lap. She felt sick; she was sure the floating thing was the body of a cow. Mark and Father had not seen it. They were staring across the Broad at the Foulgers' cottage, a small speck in the surrounding flood.

"That's where we rowed last night, Dad," said Mark, pointing his finger at the roof. "Jim had to cut a great hole in the thatch to get Hepzie out. And then Jim and I rowed back along by the Pickerel Inn to the church. It was fun, wasn't it, Mary? And all sorts of things went rushing past us in the water—masts and spars . . ."

"And a crate of oranges," added Mary, trying to rouse herself.

"And a great lump of yellow stuff like vaseline."

"Jim said it was oil."

"And all the time Canon Crowfoot and Ned Brewster were making the bells go like anything."

"They were ringing the victory sign, Hepzie said."

"Di, di, di, dump," boomed Mark.

He jumped up and down in the back of the car, in the excitement of telling his story. But Mary, though she tried to look cheerful, just ached and ached. She could not forget Myrtle's white, strained face, or the great gash in Mrs. Beamish's head, or the empty place in the village street.

She looked out at the whirling snow and bit her lip.

"Bless me!" exclaimed Dr. Vaughan as he turned into their drive. "You never really know the lie of the land till you get a flood like this."

The gravel was dry and firm. It was not until they had passed the paddock that it began to feel spongy, and not till they drew up at the surgery door that they were standing in an inch of water. Mark jumped out of the car and splashed excitedly into the house.

Each one of them hurried to that part of their home that was most precious to him. Dr. Vaughan stamped around his little consulting room, trying to get his feet warm, muttering, "It might have been worse. It might have been worse."

The sterilizer and the case of instruments had stood above the flood and so had the locked cupboard of poisons and drugs, which he kept on an upper shelf. Only the drawers of cotton wool and the pile of old medical magazines on a bottom shelf were ruined past repair.

Mark had hurried to the playroom to see if his museum had survived the flood. Like his father he, too, was lucky. When he burst into the room the stuffed bittern he had bought at Christmas from Tilney, the gunsmith, stared at him disdainfully from its cracked glass case.

"Thank goodness you're all right," he exclaimed aloud.

But poor Mary stood in anguish in the middle of the drawing-room floor, Catty perched on her shoulder, gripping hard with his claws. Last night, when they had set out to rescue the Foulgers, they had left both doors of the French windows wide open, and into the room had floated the flotsam and jetsam of the flood. Broken bits of dead reed stems and river weed lay strewn all over the floor, and, beneath them, from skirting board to skirting board, stretched a thick carpet of greenish-brown river mud. As the flood had gone down, this slime had streaked itself down the bottom eight inches of the wall, down the frills of the loose covers on the chairs, down the piano legs and the sides of the bookcase.

It was horrible. Disgusting. Foul. From the drying puddles on the floor rose a sickening, dead, watery smell, like the smell of the Reedsmere mud flats when the tide was out.

Mark came in from the playroom.

"What a dreadful stink! I say, what's that?"

He dived under the sofa and pulled out a sodden bundle of fur.

"It's a dead coypu, I think." Then turning to the open door he shouted to his father, "Come quick, Dad. I think we've got a coypu."

Mary shuddered. She hated dead things.

Dr. Vaughan stood in the doorway.

"It's a wonderful specimen, Dad. A female. Must have been drowned in the flood. I wonder if Tilney could stuff it for my museum."

But Dr. Vaughan looked past his son at his daughter's face.

"Put the creature in the toolshed, Mark," he said quietly, "and don't talk about it for the next three hours."

Then he lifted off Myrtle's cat, put his arm around Mary's shoulder, and propelled her gently out of the room.

"People before places," he smiled. "And warmth before cleaning up mud. I want you and Mark to go up to the loft and bring down anything dry you can find to burn. I'm going to put on the kettle for some tea. Then I'm going to fill the coal scuttle and light the stove in the spare room."

"The spare room!" they both exclaimed.

"Yes, my dears, the spare room. It's on the first floor."

"You mean we may expect the flood back again?"

"Yes. Until that breach in the sea wall is filled, we're at the mercy of every high tide. Now, quick, both of you. We're all shivering, and shivering isn't good for our courage."

In ten minutes flags of flames were waving behind the panes of the coal stove, and Mark and Mary and the doctor and the cat were enjoying the warmth that was slowly creeping through the room. Catty had finished a saucer of milk and was contentedly licking his white front paws. Mary poured out the tea.

"I'll have to go back to the Rest Center in a minute or two," said Dr. Vaughan.

"Can't *we* do something?" asked Mark.

"It's awfully boring staying here by ourselves doing nothing," added Mary.

"Mother and Myrtle should be back before long. You'll have to make up a bed for Myrtle."

"That won't take two minutes. Can't we do something else to help?" asked Mary.

Dr. Vaughan looked at their two flushed, sleepy faces and smiled.

"Don't worry," he said. "I've got a full program worked out for you both. After Myrtle's bed, the next item is SLEEP."

"Sleep!" they cried in disgust.

"Yes, sleep. Your mother and I are used to nights being turned into days. A doctor and a nurse have to accustom themselves to such things. But you are young. Without sleep, you're useless. And, in fact, we've got to make the greatest possible use of you both in the coming few days."

"But, Dad," sighed Mark miserably. "We've got to go back to school tomorrow."

"*Got* to, Mark? Do you want to go?"

"Of course not!" they both shouted at once.

"Can we really be any good, Father?" asked Mary excitedly.

"What can *I* do?" asked Mark.

"Come to the window on the stairs, and I'll show you."

They trooped out into the passage. The window at the top of the stairs faced east. Looking out through the bottom panes, they gazed over the top of the kitchen garden, across the flooded marsh where they had rowed last night, till their eyes came to rest on the eastern rim of the horizon—the low ridge of the Marram Hills. Inevitably they all looked northward to the breach. Under the low, shifting clouds, the water heaved, black and forbidding. Now that the flood was receding, little islands of grassy tussocks were emerging in the marsh, poking up forlorn, shaggy heads into the swirling snow.

"Not a soul to be seen," said Dr. Vaughan.

"And not a bird!" exclaimed Mark. "Where can they have all blown to?"

"In a few hours' time," said Father, "that narrow spit of the

Marram Hills will be busy with people coming and going—all the men from the village with spades, trucks with sandbags, a platoon of soldiers, perhaps. I don't know if Reedsmere is important enough for the help of the army."

"How'll the trucks get there?"

"Down the road toward Caister, and then left, past the old pill box, and then up on to the top of the Marram Hills. They'll have to lay down a track I should think, or the trucks will get stuck in the sand."

"Well, what do *we* do, Dad?"

"You can see for yourselves that ours is the nearest house to the breach. Those men working to close the gap will be at it all night, I expect. They'll be working by arc lights. They'll get cold and hungry. They'll want hot tea, Mary, and if your cooking and Mother's pantry can run to it, a hot stew. Some of the soldiers may even be billeted here. I want you to make up every bed in the house. Bring down the camp beds and the sleeping bags from the attic. If the soldiers don't use them, I am quite sure I shall find families from the village who will want to sleep in them."

"Yes, but what can *I* do?" asked Mark impatiently.

"You're as strong as an ox, Mark. You can help the men fill the breach."

"Hurray!"

"And as that ugly swell in the Broad subsides you can go down to the lodge gates and fetch *Donovan* back. It'll be useful to transport Mary and her stews."

"But Father . . ." began Mary.

Mark blushed furiously. He looked as though he were going to burst into tears.

"I've lost *Donovan,* Dad."

"Lost *Donovan?* How?"

"I tied the wrong sort of knot, and the boat floated away while Jim and I were trying to get Dotty Dick off his roof."

"Bless me, Mark," said Dr. Vaughan, looking at his son over the top of his glasses. "What an idiotic thing to do!

Never mind. It'll turn up stranded somewhere near the breach."

"Do you still think I'm any good, Dad?"

The doctor looked down in surprise.

"Any good, Mark? Of course you are!"

He put an arm around both his children.

"Your mother and I are very proud of you both," he said quietly. "I don't think we shall ever forget what you did last night."

Suddenly they were startled by the telephone bell.

"Well, that's one good thing," said Dr. Vaughan, as he ran downstairs. "They've got the telephone working again pretty quickly."

Mark and Mary listened inquiringly to one side of the conversation that followed.

"Dirty brownish-green?" asked Father. ". . . yes, that's clearly what's happened . . . You must boil it. Yes, at least seven minutes. And then filter it through silk or muslin. Tell everyone you see. I'll ring the Medical Officer of Health. Don't forget. Bring to the boil and let it go on roaring for at least seven minutes."

Dr. Vaughan put down the receiver.

"What's the matter, Dad?"

"Flood water in the mains, I'm afraid."

"What about the tea we've just drunk?"

Dr. Vaughan smiled.

"Don't worry, Mark. It was the first water to be drawn out of the tank. It's only now that the flood water will have started flowing in upstairs."

"So I must boil all the water for cooking, Father?" asked Mary.

"Yes, my dear. Do it very thoroughly, and strain it through an old petticoat or something. If you and Mark get very thirsty, drink cider. I believe Mother keeps some in the pantry."

After he had rung Mrs. Milligan at Thirlsthwaite exchange and told her to put all calls for him through to Sir Bartlett Speke, Dr. Vaughan bade them good-bye and hurried out of the house.

Mary smiled as she watched the car disappear up the drive. As usual, her father had forgotten to shut his door. It swung to with a bang as he turned sharp left by the privet hedge.

Turning back into the house, she felt daunted by its emptiness and silence and by the dreadful smell of the slime from the drawing-room floor.

She shivered. Her eyes had an odd shut-in feeling, as though they were lying dark and dull at the bottom of deep hollows and, despite the warmth of the tea somewhere just below her ribs, her legs and arms felt stiff and cold.

"It was jolly uncomfortable on the Long Room floor," she thought. "All my bones came through at the joints."

She went into the kitchen and put on a kettle of muddy water to fill a bottle for Myrtle's bed; and then, pinching her nose between the fingers of her left hand, she picked her way across the drawing-room floor to the piano. She tried to play a scale. It was just as she had feared. The keys stuck horribly, and the notes were out of tune.

Going upstairs with Myrtle's bottle, she found Mark on the window sill, gazing miserably across the marsh.

"I can't think what's happened to them, Mary. Where do moorhens and coots and grebes and water rats and coypu families go when there's a flood? Some of the coypus must be having their babies now. Do you think they're all drowned?"

"I don't know, Mark. I really don't know."

She saw that her brother looked taut and white, as he had looked rowing back from the Marram Hills last night.

"But I think we're dreadfully tired," she said. "Perhaps it'll all look better when we've had a sleep. Come along."

They had left the draft on at the bottom of the coal stove,

and the whole thing was ticking away with heat. The windows glowered fierce and orange from the glow of the coal inside. The warmth of the room closed around them.

Mary turned off the draft and stayed for a moment to tickle Myrtle's cat under his chin. He was lying with his face turned upward resting on his paws, his lips half open in a beatific grin.

"I don't think I've been really warm," she sighed comfortably as she snuggled under the spare-room eiderdown, "since the wash of *Donovan* put out the drawing-room fire. Do you remember how it hissed?"

But Mark said nothing. He was already asleep.

Ned

Up at the Rest Center after the Morning Service, the mothers of young children were trying to bring some sort of order back into their families' disordered lives.

Mrs. Brewster turned to her eldest son.

"Ned," she said, "since yer dad en't here to help us, yew'll hev to do the best yew can to tek his place."

Ned looked dubiously at his youngest brother bawling lustily in Lady Speke's wash basket, his baby fists clutching hard at the huge blanket in which he was wrapped and his red face puckered up in rage.

"It's that back tooth o' his acomin' through," his mother explained. "He want his bone ring, Ned. And Mavis want her thick coat. And June want her tin o' sweets. And I want the two pillows from our bed."

A look of surprised relief shot across Ned's face.

"Yew like me to go back home, Mum?" he grinned. "And see what I can fetch?"

"That's it, Ned."

Ned put the three middle fingers of his left hand into his mouth and let out a long shrill whistle, which, a moment later, was answered by a similar shrill screech, coming from the back of the Long Room gallery.

"We're off down the street," yelled Ned to Jimmy Bell.

They set out with a fine clatter.

118

They found one of Ben Blaza's old rowboats down at Hollow Bottom and rattled the oarlocks and boat stretchers into their place and pushed off, excitedly chattering to each other.

"Wonder what yer bungalow'll be like," remarked Ned.

"Terrible, Ma said," replied Jimmy Bell. "Two feet o' water in every room, she said. Yer house won't be no better. Yer lower down the street."

They rowed down the lower road with the tops of the hedges on either side still tossing and creaking in the last hours of the dying gale, their hands and faces stung by the cold air.

"Better fun doin' this than stayin' with all them squallin' kids," said Ned, stopping for a moment to blow on his frozen knuckles.

"Never did like babies," observed Jimmy. "Sort of selfish, bawlin' away like that. Don't give yew a chance to think."

"Cor, what d'yew want to think for?"

"Well, yew know what I mean. They stop yew from doin' anythin' but wonderin' when they're goin' to shut up."

But as they paddled down Reedsmere Street, the two boys became strangely quiet. Their village stood there, up to its knees in the flood—stone dead. Not a wisp of smoke curled up into the air anywhere, and not a sound came from the empty houses. Everyone's home seemed suddenly to have lost its privateness; with the washing away of fences, everyone's front garden had become part of the village street.

They tucked the handles of the oars under their knees and let the boat float noiselessly past the Peacheys' cottage and along the high wall of Mrs. Poyser's orchard. In the stillness, the faintest little noises came to them—the soft lapping of water flowing slowly back into the Broad, the distant dipping of other oars far down the street, the cry of a seagull away over the marsh, the sighing of the wind through a shattered pane of glass.

Gliding around the corner, they came in sight of the Bells'
bungalow.

"There it is!" exclaimed Jimmy.

And the two boys lowered their oars and gave four such
long, vigorous strokes that, before they knew what they were
doing, the boat was rushing through the tops of Mr. Bell's
Brussels sprouts.

"Steady on," yelled Jimmy, "or we'll go through the front
window."

They flattened their noses against the cold glass and
stared in.

The Bells' front parlor was in a terrible mess. The bamboo
whatnot with the fern on top had been knocked sideways on
to the settee; the chair covers clung dripping to the up-
holstery underneath, and the new flowered wallpaper was
splashed and streaked with river slime.

"It's goin' down," said Ned, trying to be comforting. "Look,
it's flowin' out under the door into the passage."

But Jimmy did not seem overconcerned by what he saw.

"Funny thing," was all he said, "the way Ma's ornaments
are sittin' up quite straight there on the mantelpiece!"

"What did she ask you to bring back?" Ned inquired.

"Nothin'."

"Nothin'?"

"No. Didn't tell her I was comin'. She's got Dad to look
after her."

"Then we'd better get goin' to our place," said Ned, sitting
down on the seat and picking up his oar.

Past the village butcher's that had once been Jim Foulger's
fish shop, they were met by two policemen in a boat.

"Don't you go climbing about the houses on that side of
the street," shouted Will Bent, pointing to the cottages which
backed on the Broad.

"Why not?" asked Ned.

"They're not safe. Mr. Clatworthy's top floor's just given

way. You'll go and get yourself drowned if you play about down there."

"But me mum wants things out of our house," shouted Ned.

"Can't help that," growled P.C. Cattermole. "Yew keep out o' them houses. See?"

"What yew goin' to do?" whispered Jimmy.

"Row down and have a look at Myrtle's house," said Ned in a loud voice.

Jimmy looked at him with a puzzled expression.

"But her house en't there any more."

Three strokes with their oars had put them out of earshot of the two policemen.

"Silly ass," muttered Ned. "Once we're out of sight o' them coppers we can row back behind the houses, all along by the coal sheds. I'll get into our house by the back door."

When they got behind the houses they found everyone's hens perched in huddled groups on top of the coal-house roofs.

Jimmy roared with delight.

"Fancy forgettin' about the hens!" he laughed.

"They don't arf look rum," said Ned. Indeed the dozen Rhode Island Reds looked extraordinary as they stretched out their necks and squawked at the passing boat.

"There's ours on our coal house, too!" he exclaimed, as he looked along the row of back gardens. "I'll take them back to Mum."

When they reached the Brewsters' home, they found the back door wide open and the water slapping up to the bottom step of the flight of stairs. Somehow, not being a bungalow, the house looked far less at the mercy of the flood than the Bells', and as Ned ran hurriedly about upstairs from room to room, collecting the pillows and the coat his mother had wanted, he was astonished how tidy and dry everything seemed.

"If only we had a fire up here I could get the family back tonight," he thought. "There's their beds all comfortable and waitin' for them. They'd be much better off than in that Hall."

But when he splashed about downstairs, looking for the baby's bone ring and June's tin of sweets, he saw how impossible it would be for his mother to cook for them all, till the water went down.

"Gosh, I wish Dad were back," he sighed, as he gazed at the dripping kitchen shelves and the gas cooker, cluttered round with bundles of reeds and broken bits of board and wire netting torn free from the hen run outside. "He'd know where to start, Dad would."

Jimmy was trying to coax the Brewsters' hens into the boat but, becoming exasperated at last by their obstinate refusal to leave the coal-house roof, he made a sudden swoop at them with outstretched arms and sent them screeching into the air. One flew into Ned's face as he splashed out of the back door.

"Hi, there!" he shouted, grabbing a handful of feathered hen.

"Darn the things!" exclaimed Jimmy, struggling red in the face with a frightened, gobbling bird under each arm.

"I know what I'll do," said Ned, turning back into the kitchen. And he reached for the biscuit tin in which his mother kept the corn.

"Let's try this," he said, scattering a handful of corn over the floor boards of the boat.

Jimmy lowered the two indignant hens between the seats, and with the gradual dying down of squawking protest on the roof, the Rhode Island Reds, one by one, pocketed their pride and walked sedately into the boat to join their sisters, eating corn.

"Now let's be off," said Ned, grasping his oar and nudging a hen off the place on the stretcher where he wanted to put his feet.

As they passed the back of the Peacheys' cottage, Ned suddenly raised his oar and stopped rowing. He sat for a moment, listening intently, a puzzled expression on his face. Above the soft clucking of the hens, he had heard a noise which he faintly recognized but could not place.

"Hear that?"

Both sat still, waiting for the noise to come again.

There it was! A long continuous squeak that started low down in the key and rose in a crescendo to such shrill heights that it ended almost in a whistle!

"Guinea pigs," announced Jimmy.

"Guinea pigs?" exclaimed Ned. "Where on earth are they acomin' from?"

"Peacheys' place."

They paddled the boat nearer the Peacheys' back door, close up under the reed thatch, and stopped to listen again. Now the shrill call of the guinea pigs was almost overhead.

"They're up in the back bedroom," said Ned. "Do you think we should go in an' get them?"

Jimmy looked around the flooded back gardens. No other boat was about, and no one could see.

"Come on," he grinned, tying the painter to the horseshoe nailed on the side of the door.

Up the gnarled old stairs of the cottage they clumped, the urgent, hungry squeak of the guinea pigs directing their way.

"Lucky Peacheys," panted Jimmy as he reached the top stair.

"Why?"

"Ma never let me keep me pigs in the house. They allus had to live out in the shed."

From under one of the little Peacheys' beds peeped a blunt, sandy-furred nose and a pair of bright eager eyes.

"There it is!" exclaimed Ned, flinging himself across the crazy, uneven old floor.

But the guinea pig ran behind the washstand and then under the chest of drawers.

"There's another," cried Jimmy, catching sight of a stout little piebald creature by the linen basket.

They were so excited trying to catch the Peacheys' two pets and laughing so hard at the way the guinea pigs doubled back and darted away again and sat grinning at them from somewhere new, that neither of the boys noticed how much the old boards were creaking or how the whole room seemed to be swaying drunkenly from side to side.

"Got it!" shouted Ned, triumphantly holding the sandy guinea pig tight against his chest.

"So've I," came Jim's muffled voice from under the bed.

Out of the corner of his eye Ned caught sight of the iron washstand toppling over. Creak! Creak! Crash! Every piece of furniture in the room seemed suddenly possessed with life. Washstand, linen basket, chest of drawers—they were all careering madly toward the bed in the middle of the room.

"Look out!" yelled Ned. "The floor's givin' way."

But it was too late. With a rending of wood and a crash of plaster beneath, Jimmy and the bed had fallen through to the kitchen below. Before Ned could stop them, the chest of drawers and the linen basket had wedged themselves in the gaping hole that Jimmy had left behind, and up through the gaps, around their edges, rose a cloud of thick, white dust.

"Gosh!" cried Ned. "Say, Jimmy, are yew all right?"

Ned tore down the stairs and into the kitchen below. From under the bed, with his face and hair white with plaster, and his clothes soaked from the water lying on the floor, crawled an astonished Jimmy, clutching an even more astonished piebald guinea pig.

"Are yew hurt?" asked Ned, running up to his friend and helping him to his feet.

"Nope," said Jimmy, grinning and shaking the bits of plaster out of his hair.

Then the two boys looked up in dismay at the ruined ceiling. A huge hole, fringed with broken boards and thin splintered laths and loose lumps of plaster, through which

they could see the wedged chest of drawers poised dangerously overhead, confronted their astonished eyes.

"Let's get out of here, quick," said Ned, suddenly remembering the two policemen they had met in Reedsmere Street.

Three minutes later, the boat containing Ned and Jimmy
and the eight hens, and the two guinea pigs, floated out
innocently into the street. Ned had cleaned up Jimmy's
plastered face and had covered up his telltale clothes with
his own top coat; and now the motley crew were making
toward the village school.

"Let's go and peek at the silly old school before we go
back," Jimmy had suggested, even though his teeth were
chattering with cold and he felt a large bruise coming out on
his forehead.

The flood on the far side of the street had receded so far
that they ran aground by the playground chestnut tree. So,
leaving the hens in charge of the boat, the two boys, each
holding a guinea pig safely in a pocket, ran across the puddly
netball court and peered through their classroom window.

They stood in silence for a minute, looking at the rows of
solid desks ranged across the glistening floor, at the wall
maps curling slightly in the damp, and at the stove, which
always smoked, standing dead and cheerless behind Miss
Cotterel's desk. The disaster of the night seemed to have left
the school almost untouched.

Suddenly Jimmy chuckled and nudged Ned with his
elbow.

"Look at the blackboard," he laughed.

There, in her fine Chancery script, was written Miss
Cotterel's parting weekend admonition:

*"Will Sally Blaza and Ned Brewster please tidy their
lockers."*

"Fancy that standing there all through the night," thought
Ned.

"Hullo, boys. How's the school?"

Ned and Jimmy jumped back with an uncomfortable guilty sort of feeling that their misfortunes over the Peacheys' floor had followed them into the playground. But they need not have worried. It was only Canon Crowfoot, standing on his rubbish heap, looking over the top of his wall.

"It's all drained out of the school, sir," said Jimmy.

"That's bad luck, isn't it?" chuckled the Vicar. "How are your homes? Have you been back to them yet?"

"Eight inches of water in the Bells' bungalow, sir," replied Ned. "And about the same in our downstairs."

"Does your father think he can get your mother and the children back there tonight, Ned?"

"He's away. He was out with the trawlers all last week."

"That's bad. Tell your mother that Mrs. Thornhill has made up six beds here at the vicarage. She and the children can come here if she likes. Except for my study, the ground floor is almost dry, so she can cook, and wash and air the clothes, and the children can romp about the kitchen. It's wonderfully warm."

"Thank you, sir. I'll tell her."

Suddenly the Vicar caught sight of the boatload of hens.

"What on earth have you got there?" he asked.

"Mum's layers," Ned replied. "They were all huddled up on the coal-house roof."

"Where are you going to take them?"

"Up to the Hall."

Canon Crowfoot looked doubtful.

"They won't want them up there, Ned. You'd much better row the boat round to the front gate, and we'll put them in my greenhouse. Mrs. Thornhill will feed them. She's fond of poultry."

By the time the boys had deposited the hens, Reedsmere Street was dotted with boats. Husbands and fathers were shouting to one another from house to house, telling one another how their homes had fared.

"Jimmy," muttered Ned rather miserably. "I suppose we ought to tell someone about the Peacheys' floor."

"Tell Mr. Peachey when we give Nan her guinea pigs," said Jimmy.

"Yeh," grunted Ned glumly.

Keeping House

The bell of the alarm clock shattered the warm silence in the Vaughans' spare room. In Mary's dreams its strident notes fell like huge raindrops into a muddy pool. She actually saw the sound—long steel rods of rain spearing the surface of the sullen pond.

"Heavens!" she thought, now wide awake. "I've actually *seen* sound! What a beastly sound to see!"

All the time she was washing her face and tugging the comb through her hair she kept thinking how odd it was that all her life she had longed to see sound—to watch the arpeggios take flight in arabesques from inside the piano or a diminuendo suddenly flush into fading sunset shades—and that now, all uninvited, a hideous noise like the bell of an alarm clock should burst into sight.

Mark was still asleep. He lay curled up like a dormouse, with a pink flush on his cheeks and the slight crease of a frown between his eyes. His mouth lay a little ajar, and one fist clutched hard at the flowered spare-room eiderdown, as though he were still desperately grasping an oar or the frayed eaves of a reed thatch. Mary hoped that he had not lived through the nightmare of last night again in his dreams.

She slipped noiselessly out of the room and tiptoed to the stairs.

"If there's no one out on the Marram Hills, I won't wake him," she decided.

But when she reached the window and looked out into the gray winter afternoon, she saw quite clearly that much had happened while they had been asleep. Small black figures were moving backward and forward along the spit of land, bent curiously as they struggled up against the wind, and leaning backward against it as they moved south.

"Still that wind," she thought. "And still those halfhearted swirls of snow."

As she looked, she saw a truck tilted dangerously to one side, grinding its way along the tip of the ridge. Low in the sky, three seagulls were struggling upwind toward Winterton, just as she had seen them struggling in the gleam of sunshine yesterday afternoon.

Before she could turn to wake Mark, the telephone bell rang. It was Canon Crowfoot.

"Is that you, Mary? Have your mother and Myrtle come home yet?"

"No. They ought to have come, oughtn't they? I don't know what's happened to them."

"Don't worry. Hospitals always take ages. And they must have dozens of casualties from the storm last night. You two all right?"

"Fine. We've just woken up. Father made us go to bed for three hours."

"Good. Good. I've got your violin here and Mark's rugger ball. I'll be with you in half an hour's time. You couldn't give an old man a cup of tea, could you?"

"Oh, Canon Crowfoot, I'd love to, but we haven't got any water. It's all green and brown and horrid. Father says the flood water has got into the mains. I don't think any tea I made with it would be at all nice."

She could hear the Canon chuckling.

"Have you tried the rain barrel outside your tool shed door?"

"I never thought of that!" exclaimed Mary.

"Nor did I," laughed Canon Crowfoot, "till Mrs. Thornhill reminded me of ours. She actually made me rain-water coffee after our Sunday lunch. Wasn't bad at all. Skim off the bits of moss that get into it from the roof, you know, and boil it well."

As Mary put down the receiver she saw a tousled Mark peering through the stairs window. He looked both excited and rather cross.

"Look, Mooney, they're all out there without me. Why the dickens didn't you wake me earlier? It's nearly three."

He pushed past her and ran into the scullery for his Wellington boots. Then he made a dash for the back door.

"But, Mark, you must have an overcoat."

"Bother."

"And some gloves."

"Don't be such a stupid mollycoddler."

He was beginning to run up the drive.

"You're forgetting the shovel," Mary shouted after him.

He turned back to the tool shed with a face of thunder, as though it were Mary's fault that he had forgotten it, and later stumped up the drive with the shovel over his shoulder and a tremendously determined set to his shoulders.

"He looks," she thought, "like a cross between Captain Scott setting out for the South Pole and one of the road men mending the Norwich–Yarmouth road."

Mary wanted to giggle. Quite clearly things were getting back to normal.

Mary put clean sheets and pillow cases on the spare beds, made up the bed in her father's dressing room, dragged down the two inflatable mattresses and the sleeping bags and the two camp beds from the attic, and then stood in a heap of equipment in the middle of the landing, wondering where to put all their guests for the night.

"Two in Mark's room. Two on the landing," she decided after much thought. "That'll be eight extra people with the two in the spare room, the one in Father's dressing room and Myrtle in the bed next to me. Hope the blankets and sheets won't give out."

She struggled rather crossly with the camp beds and pinched her fingers in stretching the canvas over the wooden frames; and then she raided the chest on the landing for car rugs and extra cushions.

"Huh! How I hate the smell of moth balls," she thought as she sneezed violently over the linen bags in which her mother stored her woolen things.

Then, thinking of an evening meal and of a fresh hot-water bottle for Myrtle's bed and of Canon Crowfoot's cup of tea, she ran downstairs, her pinched fingers throbbing.

She heated the oven, washed up the breakfast things, and mopped down the kitchen floor with a bucket of rain water to which she added a small bottle of disinfectant from the shelf in the surgery. The stink from the drawing-room floor was so repulsive that she had an overmastering desire to be clean. But an entire bottle of disinfectant was a mistake. She realized that immediately. The kitchen smelled like a hospital.

"Goodness, I hope it won't ruin the pork," she thought, hurrying the Sunday joint into the oven.

Then she ran out to the rain barrel and filled a large jug of water, which she filtered through the gravy strainer into the kettle, and filled a second bucket for water in which to peel and to boil the potatoes. She thought that she ought to give everyone five potatoes each, but by the time that she got to the twelfth her hands were not only numb with cold but also extremely dirty. The brownish red mud from her fingers had streaked the potatoes she had already peeled.

"How on earth does one get them clean when one has so little water?" she wondered.

Then suddenly, having a bright idea, she ran upstairs to find the dishtowel she had knitted for Hepzie for Christmas, but which she had forgotten to give her. Wrapping the peeled potatoes securely in the dishtowel, she ran out to the rain barrel and swished them up and down till they were clean.

"They'll have to fill up with bread," she thought, as she looked at the meager twelve potatoes lying at the bottom of the saucepan. "And if I'm to do the cooking for long, then we're all going to eat rice. After all, it's what the Chinese do. A handful of rice a day. How easy!"

By the time Canon Crowfoot arrived, the pork was sizzling, the kettle spouting steam, and Mary racking her brains about what to give such a huge party for a pudding.

Canon Crowfoot's dark figure blotted out the gray light from the kitchen window as he passed, and the next moment he almost rode into the kitchen table through the open door. Mary ran to help him. With the violin standing up awkwardly in his bicycle basket, a shovel strapped to the cross-bar, and Mark's rugger ball clutched beneath one arm, he was more than usually encumbered with other people's cares.

"Not much better on a bicycle than I am in a car, eh, Mary?" He smiled as he dismounted stiffly from the tall and ancient Rudge Whitworth that his father had given him in 1903.

"What's happened to your car?"

"Water in the ignition." Canon Crowfoot suddenly looked doubtful. "Does that sound sensible, do you think, Mary?"

"I don't know anything about cars."

"Nor do I. All I know is that the poor thing has been sitting up to its hubs in the flood all night and that now it won't start."

As Mary made tea, he looked around the kitchen, wrinkling his nose in an inquiring way.

"What an extraordinary smell you've got here!"

Mary blushed.

"I've been silly with the disinfectant, that's all. I couldn't bear the smell from the drawing-room floor. It's covered with slime from the flood."

"River ooze and dead fish, I know. It's horrible. My study's like that. The whole of Reedsmere Street is covered with it. I suppose we shall get used to it in time."

Canon Crowfoot had ridden through the kitchen door looking blue and old and full of angles, but as they sat over the spare-room fire drinking tea, he began to thaw back into his usual self.

"Your father is doing a wonderful job at the Rest Center," he said. "I've just come from the Hall. Half the village is back on his hands up there."

"How's Hepzie? How's Jim?"

"Hepzie's a bit stiffer than she usually is. And Jim? I don't know about Jim. Your father has made him go to bed."

"Why, what's the matter? He isn't really ill, is he?"

She could not imagine the gay, boisterous Jim who had rowed with them over the Broad last night staying meekly in bed at Father's command unless he were very ill.

"I think your father suspects pneumonia."

"How awful!"

Mary was silent for a moment, reliving in her imagination the dreadful hour that Jim and Mark and Dotty Dick had spent on the crumbling thatched roof.

"Don't tell Mark," she exclaimed suddenly. "He feels such a fool already, and he'll feel really awful if he knows he's made Jim ill."

"Pneumonia is the sort of thing that happens to anybody at any time, Mary," replied Canon Crowfoot, trying to comfort her. "You musn't blame Mark, or let Mark blame himself. I'm sure no one else does."

Mary smiled back gratefully.

The Vicar rose from his chair and straightened his shoulders.

"I must be off now to the breach. That's where I shall meet Mark, isn't it?"

Mary nodded.

As she watched him stiffly mount his tall bicycle and ride off, blustered by the wind, she thought he looked far too old for an hour's heavy digging, filling sandbags.

"He'll go and strain something," she thought. "As Grandfather did when he suddenly decided to chop down the oak tree."

As she entered the house the telephone bell rang again. It was the Medical Officer of Health. Mrs. Milligan had evidently forgotten to put the call through to the Rest Center.

"Dr. Boumphrey speaking. Dr. Vaughan's house? Yes? His daughter? Good. Will you give your father a message, please? It's important. Tell him I'm gravely concerned about our water situation and that I have rung Regional Headquarters. They are sending us water from Cambridge. A convoy ought to reach this neighborhood tonight. Tell him I'll ring him this evening when I know further details."

As Mary waited for Mrs. Milligan to put her through to the Rest Center, she had an absurd vision of thousands of people carrying cups of water to them across Newmarket Heath and along the straight roads toward Thetford.

Dr. Vaughan answered the telephone.

"Father, Dr. Boumphrey has just rung here. He says he's very worried about our water, and that they are sending us some from Cambridge. It ought to arrive tonight."

"Good. That'll make things a lot easier here. Have Mother and Myrtle come back yet?"

"No," replied Mary. She was beginning to feel anxious. "They're an awful long time away, aren't they?"

"Yes, but the whole county's in chaos. I expect they're worked off their feet at the hospital. How many beds have you made up, Mary?"

"Eight. We've got seven of them empty."

"I've just been in touch with the army. They're making their own arrangements about accommodations, so I'm going to send two families from here. I want young Mrs. Thrower and her husband to have the spare room. Can you think up something for the baby?"

"What sort of thing?"

"A cot. Something for it to sleep in. A large bottom drawer padded with a pillow and a thick blanket will do if you can't find anything better. They'll be coming as soon as I can get them to you. They want warmth and quiet."

"How's Jim, Father?"

"Early stages of pneumonia, I'm afraid. That reminds me, Mary. I'm sending Ned Brewster on his bicycle. Give him the bottle of penicillin in the surgery. You'll find it on the top shelf."

Mary ran up to the attic. She had suddenly remembered the doll's cot that Tom Wright, the boat builder, had made for her when she was three years old. She would love to see Mrs. Thrower's baby lying in her old doll's cot. But when she had unearthed it from behind the trunks and suitcases and the last trays of slightly shriveled apples, the Cox's orange pippins, she was assailed with doubts. How big exactly was a week-old baby? Would what fitted into a bottom drawer fit into Tom Wright's cradle? She doubted it. And she sadly tucked the doll's cot back among the lumber and went downstairs to air a pillow and a blanket and to prepare the far less romantic empty drawer.

Then there was the evening meal to think about. How was she going to feed her family, the two Throwers and five other people and Myrtle on their own Sunday joint and those twelve miserable muddy potatoes? She wished her mother would come home. Everything was getting too complicated.

"Ah well," she sighed wearily. "It'll have to be those handfuls of rice straightway."

And she ran downstairs, filled a large saucepan with filtered water from the outside rain barrel and threw in twelve handfuls of rice—one for each person sleeping the night in the house.

As dusk was darkening into night Ned Brewster arrived.

"Come for the penicillin, Mary," he shouted from the back door.

"I know. Come in while I get it. There's a fire upstairs. You look frozen."

Mary sat on the floor with Myrtle's cat in her lap and watched the warm firelight bring the color back into Ned's freckled face.

"How's Jim Foulger?" she asked.

"Dunno. He's lyin' in bed with his eyes shut."

"Doesn't sound like Jim, much."

But Ned could not keep his mind on Jim for long.

"Dad's back," he announced happily.

"Why, where's he been? Wasn't he here last night?"

"Nope. Been out with the trawlers all week. Got back this afternoon. We'll soon get the house straight, Dad and me."

"You've been back to the village? What's it like?"

"Eight inches of water in our downstairs this morning. 'Spect its lower now. And some of the houses all bashed about and crumbling up."

Then Ned told Mary about the Peacheys' guinea pigs and Jimmy falling through the floor and the dreadful mess they had left behind.

"Well, you couldn't help it," said Mary consolingly. "You had to save the guinea pigs."

"Mr. Peachey didn't think so," said Ned ruefully. "He weren't arf mad when we told him."

Ned went off with the medicine, and, as Mary came back through the kitchen, she saw that alarming things were happening on the gas stove.

"Heavens! The rice!" she exclaimed.

It had swollen and swollen, and was rising up out of the saucepan in a great frothy mess. She quickly poured off half into a second pan.

Two minutes later, Mark burst into the house.

"I've brought *Donovan* back," he announced triumphantly. "Guess where I found her?"

"Can't imagine."

"No. Guess. Guess. Guess."

"On the roof of the Pickerel Inn," hazarded Mary wildly.

"No. Wedged in the door of Hepzie's wash house. I went over from the breach to have a look at the cottage, and there she was, just waiting for me. Nothing broken. Oars quite safe."

"What was the cottage like?"

Mark wrinkled up his nose.

"Disgusting. Much worse than the drawing room. The

mud's right up to the ground floor ceiling; and the garden's full of sand and pebbles and mess."

"Poor Hepzie."

"Oh, Mooney," went on Mark, his face bright with excitement. "It was wonderful out by the breach. You must come tonight. They're rigging up lights now. We'll go by boat and take your stew and some bits of wood to make a fire to heat it up. I've found a place out of the wind and a couple of bricks to balance it on."

"Oh, Mark!" wailed Mary. "The stew!"

"What's the matter with it?"

"I've forgotten all about it. That's all."

"You are a fool."

"I don't think it's too late. Let's see what we can put into it."

They ran to the storage cupboard and each chose the canned food he liked best. Mark came out with three cans of corned beef and five cans of baked beans. Mary chose sweet corn, garden peas, and Irish stew. When they had poured them all into their mother's largest saucepan, a huge iron one they had once used for boiling up scraps for the hens, Mary began to feel doubtful.

"Do you think all those things'll mix?"

"Doesn't matter if they don't. It's so cold out there and people are working so hard, they'll eat anything."

"It's very stodgy looking. How can we make it wet?"

"Soup," suggested Mark. "Cans of soup."

So they poured in three cans of tomato soup and two of mulligatawny and stirred the concoction as it heated up on the stove.

"Smells all right," said Mark, clearly proud of the result.

By this time the rice had started swelling again, and Mary had to pour some more off into a third saucepan.

"If it doesn't stop swelling soon," she thought, "the whole kitchen will be full of rice."

Good News

Myrtle sat on the spare room hearth mat, tickling Catty under his chin, and talked and talked and talked.

"Yes, and we felt awfully grand, didn't we, Mrs. Vaughan? There we were, stuck behind all them trucks and things, and suddenly the driver rang the ambulance bell and shot straight out on the right-hand side of the road. And we raced past the policeman and the traffic lights, clang, clang, clang, as though the whole of Reedsmere was on fire."

The firelight gleamed in her bright eyes.

"And it were only yer mum and me in the ambulance, Mary," she laughed. "No one sick, at all!"

It was wonderful to have Myrtle back with the frozen horror gone from her face.

They had burst out with their good news almost before they were out of the car. Mrs. Beamish was not seriously hurt. The X ray had revealed no fracture of the skull. She was suffering from concussion and exposure, and needed warmth, rest, and absolute quiet. She might be back in the village in a week.

"Yew never saw such a lot of stuff on the roads," continued Myrtle gaily. "Soldiers and ambulances and police and trucks of sandbags and lots and lots of those oil tankers."

"Not oil!" exclaimed Mary. "It's water. They're bringing us water. I'm sure that's what they are."

And she told Myrtle and her mother about the flood getting into the mains, and how drinking water was being sent from Cambridge.

"And then there were people just out for the lark of it," Myrtle went on. "People in little cars and on motor bikes, and two on a tandem, there were—come to see what we all looked like after the flood."

"The sea has broken through the defenses all down the coast," Mrs. Vaughan explained to Mary and Mark.

"From Mablethorpe right down to Canvey Island," added Myrtle.

"Where's that?" asked Mark.

"Somewhere down Essex way, en't it, Mrs. Vaughan?"

Mrs. Vaughan nodded.

"And Wroxham's in a terrible mix. All the traffic jammed for nearly a mile at that crossroads, and the boats all floating out of the boat houses and lyin' about in the fields, and the town full of planks and spars and oars and things. And Thirlsthwaite's even worse. The road's still under water."

"Have you been through our village yet?"

"No," said Mrs. Vaughan quickly. "The ambulance dropped us at the Hall and we came on here by the Thirlsthwaite road in Father's car."

"Why didn't you bring Mrs. Thrower and her baby?" asked Mary. "Father wants them to sleep the night here. Look, I've made the baby a cot out of the bottom drawer."

And she showed them all the preparations she had made for the night.

"It looks like a nice, friendly, untidy sort of hospital," said Myrtle.

"You've done wonders, darling," exclaimed Mary's mother.

"But I still can't understand why you didn't bring the Throwers," Mary said. "Father was so insistent that they wanted warmth and quiet quickly."

Mrs. Vaughan looked at her watch. It was six o'clock.

"We'll see what happens in the next hour," she said. "If all's well then, I'll drive back to the Hall and pick up the Thrower family and Father and bring them back to supper."

"I don't understand. What *can* happen in the next hour?"

"High water's at six forty-seven, Mooney," said Mark in his most matter-of-fact voice.

"And you think that the flood will come back?"

"No, I don't think it will," replied her mother. "It's only an ordinary high tide. But it's no good taking any risks. I want you to go down the garden, Mark, and tell me how far up the lawn the water has got to. Take the flashlight from the car."

"And if the flood does come back?"

"We'll all pack into the car and drive up to the Hall."

"It's not tonight that they're worried about down at the breach," put in Mark. "It's the night of February fifth. Thursday night. Mr. Blaza said we'd just got to get the breach mended by then or the sea'd be right up to the Hall next time."

"Isn't it wonderful that Mrs. Beamish is not so badly hurt as we thought," said Mary to her mother, when they were alone.

Myrtle was in the bathroom, trying to wash herself in rain water drawn from the tool-house barrel.

"Yes, it's a miracle, darling. But they've both got a hard time ahead of them. It'll take courage to get themselves back on their feet."

"How do you mean?"

"They've got nothing left in the world except each other and Catty and the clothes they stand up in. Even if the Council starts building immediately, they won't have a home for months."

"They must stay here," exclaimed Mary.

Her mother smiled.

"I'm glad you said that. It's just what I've been thinking. I shall love to have them. The house always seems dreadfully empty when you two have gone back to school."

"When the Throwers go, you can turn the spare room into a little apartment for them. Oh dear, I wish I was going to be here. It would be such fun having Myrtle in the house."

Mrs. Vaughan wrinkled her forehead in an effort to remember where they were in the week.

"It's tomorrow, isn't it?"

"Tomorrow what?" broke in Mark as he burst through the kitchen door.

"That you go back to school."

"No, we don't. No, we don't. No, we don't," he shouted, leaping around the kitchen table in a mad kind of tribal dance.

"Father says we can stay and help," put in Mary excitedly. "Mark's to help mend the breach and I'm to stay and make stews."

A look of pained remembrance shot across her face.

"Heavens!" she exclaimed. "The rice! Please tell me what to do about the rice."

Mother and daughter contemplated the three saucepans of rice in silence for a few moments. They had just boiled dry and were beginning to smell.

"Scrape off the top two inches and mix it with butter," suggested Mrs. Vaughan calmly. "With luck no one will notice anything odd. How's the joint?"

"Spitting like a wild cat."

They opened the oven and peered in.

"Looks all right. What about a vegetable and a pudding?"

Mark suddenly burst out laughing.

"You've both forgotten the flood," he shouted.

"Where's it got to now?" asked his mother.

"Your yellow tree peony."

"And the time?"

"Six twenty-five."

"Then we're all right aren't we, Mark? Only another twenty minutes for it to rise. It can't reach the house in that time."

"The postman's bag!" shouted Myrtle from the top of the stairs. "Oh, Mrs. Vaughan, I've forgotten the postman's bag!"

They all ran out of the kitchen into the hall and looked up at Myrtle, standing there in distress. She was wearing an old pair of Dr. Vaughan's pajamas that Mrs. Vaughan had laid out for her.

"And it's got the cash book and the postal orders and all the petty cash in it!" she wailed.

The pajamas were so long in the sleeves and legs that Myrtle could not find her hands and feet and was scarcely able to move. She looked like a very young, unhappy clown.

"Ma set such store by them," she almost wept. "She'll be that moithered if they're lost."

"Where did you leave the bag, Myrtle?"

"Up at the Rest Center. I forgot all about it when the ambulance came."

"Well, cheer up. I'm just going up to the Hall to fetch the Doctor and the Thrower family. I'll bring it back with me. Mary, roll up Myrtle's pajama legs and run upstairs and find her a pair of slippers and a dressing gown."

The two girls sat in the dark by the spare room fire while they waited for the party from the Hall to return. It was quite the best way of sitting, for, in the intimate warmth of the fire glow, thoughts were spoken aloud that would have remained unsaid had the electric light been on.

"Ma looked awful lyin' out there on the roof," whispered Myrtle. "I thought she was goin' to die."

"It must have been dreadful," murmured Mary.

"So quiet like. Never known her like it."

"But she's comfortable now."

They sat in companionable silence for a minute, enjoying

the warmth creeping up their legs and over their hands and faces. Then Myrtle began to giggle.

"Can't think what she'll say when she wakes up. Ma never did hold with bossy women like nurses."

"Perhaps they won't be bossy at all. They're sure to be very kind."

"That's it," sighed Myrtle. "She can't abide people pityin' her, Ma can't."

Mary wondered for a moment whether her mother would know how to deal with a homeless possessionless clothesless Mrs. Beamish without showing she was sorry for her. And then she turned her attention to a more immediate problem.

"What would you like to wear tomorrow, Myrtle?" she asked. "Your clothes won't be dry after Mother's washing them tonight."

"Dunno. What d'yer think?"

It was very difficult. Myrtle was so much broader and tubbier than Mary that none of Mary's clothes fitted her.

"I wonder if Mother's ski pants would fit you and one of Mark's school pullovers?"

"I'd love that," exclaimed Myrtle. "Do let's go and see."

So Mary ran into her mother's bedroom and unearthed the ski pants, and then she grabbed one of Mark's bright green pullovers out of his trunk.

Myrtle slipped out of Dr. Vaughan's pajamas and tried them on.

"Cor," she said delightedly, gazing enraptured at herself in the long mirror. "I look just like one of them advertisements for winter sports!"

"You look lovely!" exclaimed Mary excitedly. "Now brush your hair back hard as though the wind's in it, and I'll find a silly woolen cap to stick on top."

Young Mrs. Thrower looked so exhausted when the party arrived from the Hall that Mrs. Vaughan filled her a hot-water bottle and made her go to bed, while the rest of the family were downstairs, dishing up the meal that Mary had cooked.

When they returned upstairs with the plates of roast pork and buttered rice and canned peas, the baby was hicupping softly in the bottom drawer, and his mother sat up in bed in the blue wool bed jacket that Granny had left behind, looking wonderfully at peace.

Mr. Thrower was the only one of the party that seemed ill at ease. He looked awkward and worried.

"Cheer up, Tom," said Dr. Vaughan, as they carried up the bottles of cider and beer together. "Babies are wonderfully tough. And we'll soon have the color back in Molly's cheeks. There's nothing like a good night's rest."

Then followed one of the oddest indoor picnics that anyone could imagine. Mark and Mary and Myrtle sat on the floor with their plates of pork, and Mrs. Vaughan and the doctor and Tom Thrower sat up to the dressing table on the cane-bottomed bedroom chairs, while Molly Thrower smiled on them all from the bed.

"Oh, Mrs. Vaughan," giggled Myrtle with her mouth full of pork. "Isn't everythin' funny? Just think of us all sittin' up here in yer spare room!"

"I always used to think it was rather a dismal sort of room," said Mrs. Vaughan. "Now, I shall remember it as one of the nicest rooms in the house."

The wind still banged in the creeper outside, and everyone saw in his mind's eye the black stretch of the swollen Broad and the mud and wreck that the flood had left behind. Yet within those four walls, the warmth and the light from the shaded lamps and the open fire, the smell of food and the clatter of knives and forks banished the specter outside. Mary saw that the firelight glowed in Myrtle's hair and winked in Tom Thrower's golden glass of beer and flashed off her father's glasses and cast a warm flush over Molly Thrower's tired face. After the cold horror of last night, they were all touched by the joy of the fire.

Then the baby in the bottom drawer suddenly gave a loud, grown-up sneeze. And everyone shouted with laughter.

"Not as funny as the horrid mess inside your postman's bag!" announced Mark, when they were quiet again.

"The postman's bag!" exclaimed Myrtle in horror. "I've forgotten all about it again."

"The money's all stuck together with aniseed balls, and those post office papers have all run together with the melted chocolate and licorice. It tastes horrid; it's full of cat's hair."

"Oh dear, whatever shall I do?" asked Myrtle, looking comically distressed.

"Nothing tonight, my dear," said Mrs. Vaughan.

"No one can steal anything when it's in that kind of mess," Dr. Vaughan assured her with a twinkle in his eye. "We'll lock it up in the storage cupboard and forget about it till tomorrow."

Mary looked toward the bed and suddenly put her finger to her lips.

"Hush," she whispered. "Mrs. Thrower's asleep."

"And that's what you ought to be, too, Myrtle," whispered Mrs. Vaughan, putting her hand gently on Myrtle's shoulder.

An Accident

And now they were out on Reedsmere Broad in *Donovan* once more—the three of them, Father, Mark, and Mary. Dr. Vaughan rowed, Mark steered, and Mary sat in the bows listening to the water slap, slapping against the clinker boards eighteen inches below. They were all of them silent, tired by the long day's tasks; and yet kept alert and expectant by the weirdness of the scene. Seaward the arc lights gleamed on the Marram Hills, casting long, golden roads toward them over the surface of the Broad. Nearer, beside the boat, the water chopped black and sullen, and the banks of uncut reeds, now smudged with slime and weeds, rose gaunt and forbidding in the dimness.

Mary saw all these things with her eyes, yet the strange beauty of the lights and the cold grimness of the Broad only touched the top part of her mind. Deep down she was wrapped in warmth, folded round in a blanket of relief and content. Mrs. Beamish was not going to die. Myrtle was safe and sleeping in the bed next to hers. Mrs. Thrower and her baby, Father, Mother, Mark—they were all saved from the flood. Jim's illness and the state of the Foulgers' cottage were the only really serious things left to worry about.

The wind was still blowing in gusts from the northwest, so that every now and then Dr. Vaughan caught his right oar in the topmost crest of a black wavelet as he swung it back.

Mary shivered, as the spatter of drops fell over her face and coat, and pressed her legs even closer against the iron saucepan of hot stew wedged on the floor between her feet. Its warmth crept pleasantly up her calves and thighs.

Just past the dark hump of the reed stack they heard a hoarse, waterish chuckle.

"Oh, Dad, it's a moorhen!" cried Mark. "Hurray! They're back again."

In his efforts to peer through the darkness he nearly toppled out of the boat.

"Trim the boat, you donkey!" shouted Dr. Vaughan. "We don't want to go wading about in the flood again tonight."

"But Dad, I haven't seen a decent marsh bird all day—only a few seagulls this afternoon. I thought they'd all been swept out to sea."

The chuckle of the moorhen brought back to Mary all sorts of happy summer memories—of lying in the bottom of *Donovan* with the scarlet cushions and *Little Women* all one hot summer afternoon, browsing through the childhood of Jo and Amy and little Beth and listening with half an ear to the tiny clucks and swishings of grebes and coots on the surface of the Broad. She had often cast the boat off from its moorings and let it float where it would. Sometimes it was best not to read at all, but to lie looking at the sky, watching the few clouds and seeing every now and then the feathery tops of the reeds as the boat glided past a reed bank. At such times she would listen to music in her head, to Beethoven's Seventh Symphony and to Schubert's great C Major. She knew them both so well that she could "play" them to herself in her head—strings, woodwind, brass, percussion—all the instruments of the orchestra.

Now they were nearing the narrow spit of the Marram Hills and they could distinguish the dark figures crossing the beams of the arc lights and hear the men shouting to one another as they worked.

As they approached the breach, they could feel the swift moving of the water under them as it hurried out to sea.

"Don't try to cross the race, Mark," Dr. Vaughan said. "We'll moor where we can, south of the breach."

When they landed, Dr. Vaughan picked up the shovel from the bottom of the boat and strode forward to join the rest of the village. Mary and Mark carried the stew pot up the bank, walking carefully so as not to trip over the tufts of marram grass, till they came to the spot that Mark had selected for a fire. There was the little hollow he had made, and there were the bricks.

"Now let's go back to the boat for the paper and matches and the bundle of kindling," suggested Mary.

"And for that flashlight of Dad's I wore last night," said Mark. "I felt it there behind the seat with my hands when I was disentangling the rudder ropes. It may've got rusty sitting all night half out of Hepzie's wash house."

But the flashlight still worked. Mark put it over his head, and, by its light, hunted about in the boat for the matches and kindling and the dozen blue porridge bowls and picnic spoons for the stew.

"We'll have to wash up in the sea," Mary observed.

"Gosh, you don't want to worry about things like that! In the dark no one'll be able to see if you've washed up or not. And anyway, who cares?"

As they beachcombed the shore for bits of driftwood and spars and dead lupin stems for their fire, they heard the men shouting to one another.

"Did I tell yer 'bout Yarmouth, Bill?" yelled Joe Brewster, as he shoveled shingle into a wheel barrow. "They've got all that timber off the wharves floatin' 'bout the streets. 'Arf the town's under water."

"Me old missus got her ma in Yarmouth," yelled back Bill cheerfully. "House in Peggotty Street. She won't 'arf be in a moither."

"The sea's in at Bridlington," joined in another voice.

"And 'arf o' Lincolnshire's bin flooded out," shouted a third.

"Breydon Water's full of dead cows," boomed Ben Blaza as he rattled the last shovelful of stones into the heavy barrow.

When they had gathered a large enough pile of wood to keep a fire going for some time, Mary turned to Mark.

"Before we light a fire, I want to look at Hepzie's cottage. How did you get across the breach this afternoon?"

"Easy, by rope."

"By rope?"

"Come and look."

They wound their way through the men and their barrows, past the tilted truck, past their father and Sir Bartlett Speke filling sandbags from a heap of shingle, past a chain of soldiers, heaving the sandbags from man to man, till they came to the great yawning gap of the breach.

"Do you remember the wall of water and the mast hurtling through?" whispered Mary.

It was quieter now. She peered down at the waves slapping their lips.

"I can't see the rope," she said.

"Look above your head."

Above her were two stout ropes which she now saw stretched away in the darkness to the other side of the gap. Behind her the ropes sloped up about seven feet to a heavy iron tripod fixed securely in the sand dune.

"The soldiers rigged it up this afternoon," Mark explained. "You see, there were more of them working on the other side of the breach, and their lieutenant kept wanting to go from one side to the other to tell them what to do. So he sat in that cradle thing and either pulled himself across or got one of his men to. It's quite easy."

Mary saw a stout canvas belt and reins dangling from the lower rope about two feet above her head. She shuddered.

"You're not afraid, are you?"

Mary looked down at the water and then up at the canvas cradle. She bit her lip and shook her head.

"Well, you needn't go if you don't want to. I don't really

see the point of poking about the Foulgers' cottage in the dark. It's a silly idea."

But to Mary it was not a silly idea at all. Ever since she had heard that Jim was ill with pneumonia she had kept wondering what was going to happen to them both. Other people had someone young and strong to clean up their houses. Hepzie and Jim had no one. From Mark's description their cottage was in a far worse state than anyone else's in Reedsmere. She wanted to see it with her own eyes. She wanted to know if she and Mark could possibly clean it and set it to rights themselves.

"How do I get up to that cradle thing?" she asked. "It looks too high."

"We'll get one of the soldiers to help us. Once you can catch hold of it, the ropes give a bit."

Mary shuddered again.

Crossing the breach in the cradle was the most horrifying thing that Mary had done in the last twenty-four hours. She was nearly frozen with fright. Halfway across she looked down at the current slipping blackly out to sea and felt sick with alarm. As a soldier unstrapped her on the other side, she told herself that she must somehow conquer the fear.

"If I'm really going to clean up Hepzie's cottage, I shall have to go back and forwards across that rope several times a day."

It was so dark away from the arc lights that Mark and Mary held hands as they walked cautiously over the soggy marsh toward the Foulgers' cottage. In spite of Mark's glow-worm light shining from his head, they stumbled once or twice in deep, muddy holes, and the insides of their boots grew heavy with water. But at last they reached the sand-strewn slope that had once been Hepzie's garden.

They stood in the doorway looking down the beam of the flashlight.

It was awful. The walls were streaked with sandy slime,

and over the floor lay two feet of shingle. All the ornaments had been swept off the mantelpiece. The faded photograph of Hepzie's father, resplendent in mutton chop whiskers, was dripping with water. The chairs and table were pushed against the inside wall and half buried in shingle.

"Oh, Mark," wept Mary. "We'll never be able to do it ourselves. It's hopeless. It'll take dozens and dozens of men to dig all that stuff out."

"Not dozens," replied Mark, more practically. "About six, digging hard for half an hour each."

As they walked back over the marsh they puzzled out what could be done.

"If we could get them to help just a little," said Mark, "we might be able to do the rest ourselves."

"But they've got their own houses to dig out and the breach to fill," sighed Mary.

Soon, they had the fire burning between two bricks, and the surface of the stew began to heave slowly up and down. The gay rags of the flames, now curling up around the sides of the black iron pot and now, at the will of the wind, blown flat along the sand, made them both feel more cheerful.

"It smells even better out here in the night," observed Mary, as she stirred the brew with a huge ladle they had brought with them. "I hope they'll all like it."

Mark's mind had a way of taking astonishingly wide jumps, like the leaping of a kangaroo.

"Mary, do you think we could bribe them?"

"Bribe who?"

"Why, all the people who eat our stew."

"What do you mean?"

"A bowl of stew in return for five minutes' digging in the Foulgers' cottage."

"Oh, Mark, we can't do that, can we? It sounds awful."

"Why?"

"They may not like the stew."

"Someone's got to clear up that place. Shingle's awfully heavy to throw on the end of a shovel, especially when it's all mixed up with sand, and it's wet. I know. I tried it this afternoon."

The more Mary thought the matter over the more she realized that they would have to get help with the cottage. Mark's plan was not entirely impossible. She only wished she were more confident of their cooking.

"We'd better ask them *before* they eat it," she said.

"Of course."

"Will you ask them, Mark? I don't think I'd like to, much."

"Yes. I don't mind."

Now the stew was boiling hard. The old adage "a boiled stew is a spoiled stew" came into Mary's mind, and she quickly lifted the heavy pot off the bricks.

"Quick, Mark. Go and tell everyone, while I lay out the bowls and spoons."

Soon Ben Blaza and Dan Ball and Ned Brewster's father and three of the soldiers were gathered round the fire, warming their numbed hands and sniffing the night air.

"Me ole girl never makes food smell like that!" Dan Ball exclaimed.

"What's in it?" asked Ben Blaza.

"You've got to guess," replied Mary at random. She was not quite sure whether they were laughing at her or whether they really liked what they smelled, but somehow she and Mark had got to carry the thing off.

"It's a nice idea," remarked one of the soldiers kindly.

Mark cleared his throat.

"We want you to do something for us," he said. "If we give you a bowl of our stew, please will you spend five minutes tomorrow digging the shingle out of Mr. and Mrs. Foulger's front room?"

Dan Ball let out one of his gales of laughter.

"He's a caution, that boy," he bellowed to Ben Blaza.

"Lands ole Jim up on that thatch arf the night and then . . ."

But the rest of his remark got caught up in another bellow of laughter, and both of them shot south down the coast in a sudden squall of wind. Mary felt herself grow hot with discomfort.

"Where's Mr. and Mrs. Foulger's cottage?" asked the soldier quietly.

"Over there, the other side of the breach," said Mark, standing up and pointing north into the darkness. "It's only two minutes' walk from the Marram Hills."

"I know. I saw it this afternoon. We'll give you a hand, won't we, boys?" said the soldier, turning to his companions.

"Aye, Mark boy, don't you fear," added Ben Blaza as he blew on his bowl of stew. "We'll all give a hand."

"Bit of all right," mumbled Ned's father with his mouth full.

Now Dr. Vaughan and Sir Bartlett Speke had joined the group.

"I can't vouch for what's in it," their father said. "But it's at least hot."

Dan Ball gave Mark a nudge in the ribs.

"Hev Doctor and the Squire got to dig, too?"

"What's this?" asked Sir Bartlett.

"You don't git no stew, Squire," laughed Ben Blaza, "if yew don't help dig the shingle out of Mr. and Mrs. Foulger's front room tomorrow. Cooks' orders. Thems is."

Sir Bartlett looked at Mary and Mark, their faces bright in the firelight.

"Well done," he said. "I'll be delighted. Nine-thirty sharp with my shovel. Will that do?"

Mary wanted to hug him.

As they sat in *Donovan* waiting for their father to join them, Mary looked at the dying glow from their fire in its hollow of sand, and felt a new tide of happiness rising inside her. The stew had done its job, and everything was going to be all right. Hepzie's cottage would be cleaned and scrubbed and sweet again. The water was going to flow back into the sea, the mud would be shoveled away, and the Broad would echo with birds' songs and glitter with sunshine once more. "It's going to be like the old days," she thought.

But Mary was wrong. The terror and pain that the great gale had brought in its wake had not yet passed.

They were trying to move the truck, which had stood from early afternoon tilted drunkenly on the side of the sand dune. Someone in the truck was pressing down the accelerator and roaring the engine.

"It's stuck in the sand," yawned Mark sleepily from the boat. "I bet the back wheels are whizzing round and round like mad."

They both watched the dark figures of the men closing in to help shove the truck out of its skid.

Suddenly above the roar of the engine came a scream and a shout. The shouting continued, and the engine stopped.

Mary's eyes stared wide and aghast. She had never heard a grownup scream before. It was dreadful. Appalling. All the worst terrors of people suffering pain swept over her in a great engulfing tide.

"There's been an accident," gasped Mark, turning a white face to his sister.

But Mary continued to sit there in the stern of *Donovan*, paralyzed with horror. What a terrible pain it must have been to make a grownup scream!

"Mary, we've got to do something. Someone's hurt. Dad'll want help. Mary, do wake up!"

They staggered out of the boat. Mark ran forward into the circle of light in which the truck stood. But Mary stayed on the bank by the boat in the darkness. She wanted to turn south and run, run, run away into the night. Very slowly she lifted a heavy foot and forced herself to go to her father.

Dr. Vaughan was kneeling half under the truck, talking very slowly and gently to someone lying there on the sand. Suddenly he turned and looked up at the circle of gray-faced men standing round.

"We've got to lift it."

Catching sight of Mark and Mary, he beckoned to them.

"I want you two under the truck with me while they're lifting," he told them quietly. "Mark, I want you to help me pull the boy away. And I want you, Mary, to hold his hands."

Mary shook her head. Inside, deep down she was saying, "I can't. I can't. I can't."

Dr. Vaughan suddenly smiled at her.

"You can, Mary," he whispered.

It was the soldier who had said that he would dig the shingle out of the Foulgers' cottage. He was lying on his back with his eyes shut, as though he were asleep. Mary's eyes traveled slowly down his body till they came to his knees. She took a deep breath. Then she returned to his white, quiet face. Both legs just below the knees were wedged under the left back wheel of the truck. She felt calmer now. If the soldier could take this horror so quietly, so surely could she.

Father had asked for a coat to be passed down to them. By scooping away the sand, the three of them edged it inch by inch under the soldier's head and shoulders.

"Now gently. Very gently." Father murmured. "While we edge it under his hips."

Mary marveled at Mark's extraordinary nimbleness. She felt quite clumsy beside him.

"Now we're ready," said Father. "Mary, take his hands, and Mark, take hold of the rolled-up edge of the coat just here. When they start lifting the truck, watch me. We've got to work as a team."

Mary could hear Sir Bartlett Speke placing the men round the corner of the truck.

"Blaza, you here. Brewster, you beside him. Ball, you at

the back there. Now you two boys, I want you with me here."

How extraordinarily quiet and disciplined they all were! Mary saw their feet shuffle into place beside her in the sand.

"Now up with her," shouted Sir Bartlett.

And the oily bottom of the truck slowly rose above their heads.

Now that they had the soldier out under the night sky, Dr. Vaughan took off his own coat and wrapped it about his patient. It was horribly cold. Sir Bartlett Speke took off his and did the same.

Under the truck, Mary had grasped the soldier's wrists and tried to will her youth and strength down through her own veins and up into his. As they moved him, he had groaned and opened his eyes. She had smiled at him, and, when the worst of the pain had passed, he had smiled back at her. Now he lay as though sleeping again, sighing every now and then, as if his dreams were unhappy.

Dr. Vaughan stood up and looked down the Marram Hills into the darkness. Then he turned toward *Donovan,* riding at her moorings on the Broad.

"It'll have to be the boat," he said. "It's too long a journey by land, and we'll all stumble over those tufts of marram. Blaza, you've got a good stout spade there. I want you to go and knock out the front seat. I want him to lie flat along the bottom of the boat."

Mark's ears pushed back with astonishment.

"Knock out the front seat of *Donovan?* What a terrible thing to do!" he thought to himself.

"We'll get Tom Wright to fit another one, Mark," said his father with a faint smile.

Someone remembered having seen a tarpaulin lying on the floor at the back of the truck. It was just what they wanted. Very slowly, with what Mary recognized as the extraordinarily tender patience of men, they moved the soldier on to the tarpaulin and, at her father's direction, rolled the tarpaulin into a long thin sausage close up on either side of him. Then, very carefully, three taking each side, they carried him perfectly rigidly, as though on a stretcher, toward the boat. Mary shuddered. From her bedside reading of *The First Aid Manual*, she knew that this was the way one carried a patient with a broken spine.

"Mark," said his father. "I want you to run home by the sand dunes and along the road as quickly as you can. Wake Mother and tell her to phone for the ambulance. Don't risk the short cut through the marsh."

Mark turned to go, but Dr. Vaughan stopped him and added quietly so that the others could not hear.

"Tell Mother to get a hypodermic ready. She'll understand."

Sir Bartlett Speke sat in the stern and Mary, holding both sides of the boat at the bows, gently lowered herself on to the seat, as one does in getting into a canoe. She did not want to tip the boat and so give the soldier a jolt. He lay watching her, the coats tucked up high under his chin and reaching down to his feet, hiding his crushed legs. He looked apologetic, as though he were ashamed of the trouble his accident had caused.

"I shall want you all at the quay to help us lift him out," Dr. Vaughan said to the two soldiers and the three men from the village. "Go quickly. It's very cold, and we must not keep him out in the boat longer than we need."

Mary gazed at the white face, there at the bottom of *Donovan*, and her eyes filled with tears. She hoped that he would never know that she had wanted to run away down the coast.

Her father, with even more care than she had shown, put his hands on either side of the boat and delicately maneuvered himself on to the back rowing seat. They had already taken out the stretchers and, since the soldier was lying where Dr. Vaughan should have put his feet, he balanced them on the upper curves of the thwarts on either side.

"Cast off, Mary," he said quietly. And with an easy motion he pulled the boat away from the Marram Hills and out into the Broad.

Behind them they had left their shovels stuck upright in the sand, the truck still tilted on the slope, and the big empty stew pot on the bank where they had moored. At the last moment, one of the soldiers had remembered to turn off the Diesel engine which generated the electricity for the arc lights. The sand dunes and the breach lay curtained in darkness.

Cleaning Up

"Wake up! Wake up, Mooney!"

Mark had jumped on Mary's bed and was pummeling his sister hard with his fists.

"It's after ten. Mum and Dad have gone off to the Rest Center. They've left a note on the kitchen table. We're to join them for lunch."

Mary passed straight out of sleep into a most businesslike and wide-awake efficiency.

"Where's Myrtle?"

"Washing aniseed off the pennies in the kitchen sink."

"Where's Mrs. Thrower?"

"In bed, feeding the baby."

"And all those bodies in the beds on the landing?"

"All gone."

"Where?"

"Where they came from, I suppose. One's left a dirty handkerchief behind."

"Where's Mr. Thrower?"

"Oh, stop asking questions," grumbled Mark irritably. "I'm jolly hungry."

Mary sat up in bed and looked her brother up and down.

"Go and cut yourself some bread and cheese then," she said. "And if you're thirsty, open one of those bottles of cider."

Mark's mouth fell open.

"Aren't you going to cook me something?" he asked in dismayed surprise.

"Certainly not. We haven't got time."

Mary jumped out of bed and hurried into her clothes.

"Why, what've we got to do?"

"Got to do!" she exclaimed, slapping a hair brush hard down on top of her hair. "Why we've got to row across to the cottage and see what the men have done about shoveling out the shingle."

She looked about under the dressing-table mirror for her bobby pins.

"We've got barely six more hours of daylight," she continued. "And there's thousands of things for us to do. If they've cleaned out the shingle, we ought to scrub all that slime off the walls, clean the floor, and light a fire to dry the place out."

She was halfway downstairs now.

"We want a bucket and mops and firewood and soap and a bottle of disinfectant and color wash, and brushes and . . . Heavens! I've forgotten Mrs. Thrower."

She ran back upstairs into the spare room.

"Have you got everything you want for the baby?" she panted.

Mrs. Thrower looked about sixteen this morning. Her face broke into a smile.

"Tom's coming back in half an hour. He just bicycled up to the Hall to get bread and milk. You be off," she laughed. "Baby and I'll be fine."

"And we want matches and a floor cloth and a little kerosene to get the fire going and . . ."

Mark stumped downstairs behind his sister and stood in the passage looking at her in bewilderment, as she darted from one cupboard to the next, collecting all the things she had listed.

"Mooney, I think you've gone mad," he said heavily.

Mary stood and looked at him for a second, and then dashed into the pantry and picked up a loaf, a large piece of Cheddar cheese, and three rather soft Cox's orange pippins.

"Myrtle," she shouted back over her shoulder, "we're going to clean up the Foulgers' cottage. Will you come with us? It's in a frightful mess."

"Of course," Myrtle shouted back, as she tossed the money dry in one of Mrs. Vaughan's dish towels. "I'll just lock the petty cash away in yer mum's storage cupboard again. Mrs. Thrower can feed Catty when the milk comes."

"There," exclaimed Mary, emerging from the pantry and stuffing an apple into Mark's mouth. "Take all those brushes and things down to *Donovan*, and we'll follow with a bucket and some cider and our old school overcoats. Myrtle and I'll feed you as you row across the Broad."

As they set out in the poor battered boat, Mark separated from the two girls by the jagged remains of the front seat, they saw at once that the flood water was much lower than it had been the night before. Large tracts of marsh now lay uncovered. Very slowly, the landscape that they knew so well was taking shape again.

"Look!" said Mary, pointing through the snow shower. "There's Paddling Bay come to the surface."

"Paddling Bay!" exclaimed Myrtle. "So it is."

It was where they had all learned to swim. Off the Vaughan quay the water was never less than five feet deep; at high tide it was nearly eight. But at Paddling Bay, a little sandy beach shelved gently into the Broad. One always remembered it as sunny there, and the ripples came in warm and bright, and ran laughing up one's legs as one lay on the sand in the shallow water. Looking back, it seemed to Mary that hours of her childhood had been spent in that charming little bay, the air heavy with the scent of meadow sweet from the marsh behind and one's eyes darting to the glitter of dragonflies, and the rustling of birds in the reeds.

"Don't feel much like a swim today," shivered Myrtle, trying to button an old coat of Mary's across her chest.

Paddling Bay had a horribly drowned look, seen through the snow, with its yellow curve flecked with the mud and rubbish of the flood. Mary tried to forget that she had ever seen it like this; and she stepped forward through the gap of the front seat and pushed a wedge of bread and cheese into Mark's mouth.

After nearly forty-eight hours of high wind, the gale was at last blowing itself out, and the water in the center of the Broad looked so much calmer that they decided to row straight across to the Foulgers' cottage.

"There's hardly any force in the water flowing out to sea," Mark observed. "I'm sure Dad wouldn't mind us taking the boat across."

Along the Marram Hills on either side of the breach, they could see a great many people mending the sea wall, and the gap had narrowed by several feet since they had inspected it in the dark last night.

"Look at all those people in posh black coats," exclaimed Myrtle, pointing to a group moving among the diggers. "What on earth d'yer think they're doing?"

"Can't think," said Mary, as they all stared.

The soldiers and the men from the village stopped their work and straightened their backs as the group talked to them.

"Somebody grand from Norwich," suggested Mark.

Now they had run aground not far from Hepzie's gooseberry bushes.

"I do wonder if they've remembered to keep their word," said Mary as the three of them ran over the littered garden and around the side of the cottage.

"They've done it! They've done it!" shouted Mark.

Neat heaps of shingle lay piled along the front wall, and when they rushed to the open door a clean scraped floor met their eyes.

"They've done it all," cried Mary. "Oh, Mark, how wonderful of them!"

Someone had righted the two chairs and hung the rag carpet up over their backs, and on the table the diggers had placed the china ornaments from the mantelpiece, which they must have turned up with their shovels in the shingle. Only three of them were broken.

"Oh look," cried Mary. "Here's Hepzie's lovely 'Visit to Brighton.'"

It was a model in pale green china of the Regent's Pavilion. Mark was as pleased as Mary to find that it was safe. Long, long ago he had thought Bluebeard lived inside it.

"What shall we do first?" asked Mary.

"Get rid of the stink," replied Myrtle.

From the Foulgers' cottage, as from everywhere in Reedsmere, rose the fetid smell of river ooze. Though the smell hung around them all the time, it was only when someone drew attention to it that its full disagreeableness surged over them.

"It's all over the garden as well as the cottage," said Mark, wrinkling up his nose in disgust.

"And Hepzie was always particular that everything should be clean," thought Mary, remembering the scrubbed table and floor and the polished chairs and the winking brass door knobs and the line full of white washing that used to hang in the neat garden every Monday morning.

"Well, we can get the cottage nice, anyhow," broke in Myrtle. "And then we can rake up all that muck in the garden and throw it into the Broad. Come on, let's get the mops and the buckets and the disinfectant."

For the next two hours they worked very hard, carrying

buckets of Broad water up to the cottage, dosing them with disinfectant, and mopping down the ceiling and walls of the two downstairs rooms. It was a task that seemed urgently important for them all to do well, something that they could point to afterward and say, "Well, that's what *we* did to clean up the mess of the flood."

Mark, though he hated to admit it to himself, had found that he was not as strong as a man. Shoveling wet pebbles into sandbags had been both too exhausting and too boring for him the day before. Mary had realized that her genius did not lie in cooking. Besides, there was nothing left in the house to cook. And Myrtle? Having lost her home and everything that she possessed, Myrtle had a passion to build something afresh, and though cleaning out the Foulgers' cottage was not quite the same thing as creating a new home for someone, it was at least something definite and constructive, which she could see quite clearly was within the power of the three of them to finish.

When the last traces of the flood had been washed away, they rested on their broom handles and looked about them, smiling.

"Well, at least it doesn't smell beastly dirty any more," said Mary.

"No," replied Mark, sniffing the carbolic. "It just smells beastly clean."

"Now, we've got to dry the place out," said Myrtle.

Then they hurried about collecting scraps of wood in the loft over the Foulgers' wash house. When they had got the fire going really well in the old black grate, they put in lumps of wet coal from the coal stack outside. At first they sizzled and smoked, but soon they began to glow, and a faint warmth began to creep across the dank room. They banked the fire up high and then wondered what to do about the windows.

"Do we leave the windows open to let the damp that's

inside the room out?" asked Mary. "Or do we shut them to keep the damp that's outside the room from getting in?"

"I can't imagine," replied Mark.

"Open," said Myrtle, authoritatively.

"How do you know?"

"That's what Ma does on a wet Monday when she has to dry the sheets in the kitchen. All the steam goes out of the winder."

"Of course," said Mary.

So they opened the cottage windows as wide as they could and propped the doors ajar. Then they climbed up the stairs to the attic bedroom above.

The first thing that met their eyes was the huge ragged hole in the plaster and thatch that Jim had cut with Hepzie's carving knife.

"Heavens! What are we going to do about that?"

They looked up through the gap at the snow-filled sky and then down at the puddle of melted snowflakes on the floor.

"We want that tarpaulin we used last night," said Mark. "We'll ask Dad if we can have it."

As they climbed down the narrow stairs again and stood in Hepzie's steaming sitting room, Myrtle looked at the streaky glistening walls.

"Don't arf look depressin'," she remarked.

"We'll have to color-wash them," said Mary.

"A beautiful yellow," exclaimed Mark excitedly. "The color of brimstone butterflies. I've always wanted to live in a room that color."

"Certainly not," said Mary firmly.

"Why not?"

"You're not going to live in the room. Hepzie and Jim are. They must decide."

Mark was doubly disappointed.

"But that means telling them what we're doing," he complained, "and I wanted to keep it a surprise."

He had acted the scene to himself as he sloshed down the walls with the water. He would lead them both through their poor messy garden, and then suddenly fling wide the cottage door and let them see what a lovely bright home they had got.

"It'll spoil it all if we tell them," he grumbled. "Oh, Mary, I do love secrets and surprises. Don't let's tell them."

"Then we'll have to ask them in a roundabout way."

"How on earth do we do that?"

"Come on. It's lunch time," she smiled. "We'll see them both up at the Hall. You leave it to me."

Part of History

It was long past lunch time. They realized this when they had got back into the boat and were halfway across the Broad. The water looked far too dark for one o'clock, and what light there was behind the snow clouds was coming from far too low down in the sky.

"I think it's nearer three," Mary said.

"Do hope they've left us something to eat," sighed Mark.

At Hollow Bridge they saw Ned sitting on the handrail of the footbridge, waiting for them.

"What's the time, Ned?" shouted Myrtle.

" 'Bout half-past two."

"Gosh, we're late."

Ned jumped off the handrail and ran to hold the prow of the boat.

"Dad and me hev finished our place," he said.

"Oh, Ned," said Mary. "I'm so glad. So you're all back home?"

"Nope. We've got to let it dry out. Won't be back till day after tomorrow, Dad don't think."

"Then can you come with us?" Mark asked eagerly.

"Don't mind if I do."

As they walked up to the Hall they told him what they had been doing in the Foulgers' cottage. But Ned seemed disappointingly unimpressed.

"Sick of cleaning up that stinky river muck," he grunted dourly. "And like as not it'll all be back on Thursday."

"Why?" asked Mary aghast. "Has something gone wrong at the breach? They were getting on so well when we rowed past them this morning."

"Run out of sandbags. That's what they've done."

"How frightful! Can't they get more?"

Ned shrugged his shoulders.

"Dunno. P'raps the nobs from London'll be able to send more."

"Which nobs?"

"D'yer mean all them men in posh black coats we saw this mornin'?" asked Myrtle excitedly. "Were they from London?"

"Yeh. That's what Mr. Blaza told Dad."

Mary suddenly felt flat and tired and rather miserable. She had been so happy and excited with their plans for Hepzie's cottage. And now, all their work might be wasted. The flood might come back again and spoil it all.

As soon as the four of them entered the Long Room they knew that something quite extraordinary had happened in Reedsmere during the last few minutes. A golden glow hung in the air. Everyone looked as proud as peacocks.

"What on earth's happened?" thought Mary.

Someone had washed down Dotty Dick's face and slicked down his hair, and they all looked as though they had just been photographed and had not had time to take the smiles off their faces.

Miss Owles was bursting with excitement.

"We've had a visitor," she exclaimed.

The whole room waited breathlessly while Mary and Mark and Myrtle and Ned digested the news.

"A visitor? Who?"

"Guess," laughed the eldest little Peachey girl, jumping up and skipping round the room.

"Guess! Guess! Guess!" everyone shouted.

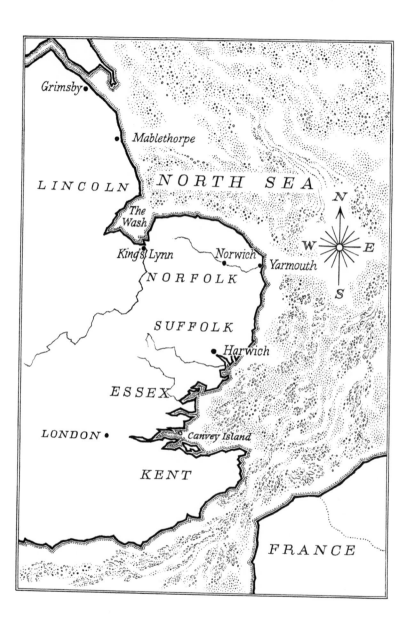

"They've all gone mad," thought Myrtle privately.

"The Mayor of Norwich," suggested Mary.

"A Rugby star," hazarded Mark.

"One of them film stars," said Ned hopefully.

"Oh, they'll never guess. They'll never guess," said the little girl. And she suddenly turned a cartwheel.

"Who can it be?" thought Myrtle.

"We give up," laughed Mary.

"The Queen!" shouted the old lady with the white hair.

"The Queen?" exclaimed the four of them.

"Yes, the Queen came to visit us," said Mrs. Lardner.

"Just after two," explained Nurse Hitchcock. "They phoned up from the Lodge to say the Queen was at the gates."

Tears were rolling down Mr. Clatworthy's cheeks.

"Like a fairy princess, she were."

"And so simple and gentle," added Miss Cotterel.

"A silk scarf over her head and warm coat," put in Mrs. Peachey.

"And she talked to us, she did," said the little girl, still pirouetting around the room. "And asked us our names and how old we were."

"And did Dad see her?" asked Mark. "And Mum?"

"No, they'd gone back home to find you," said Mrs. Lardner.

"Oh, how wonderful to see the Queen!" burst out Mary aloud.

A great lump was rising in her throat. It was joy and pride and excitement all mixed up. She looked around with new eyes at poor old Dotty Dick and silly Miss Owles and kind, fat Mrs. Lardner. The Queen had visited them! Quite suddenly, they and the whole of Reedsmere had stepped into the pages of history.

"We're important," she said breathlessly, turning to Mark. "Do you realize, we're really very, very important."

But Mark was not attending. He was looking around the Long Room with a perplexed expression on his face.

"Where's Jim?" he asked. "I hope he didn't miss the Queen, too."

"Mr. Foulger's in the billiard room," answered Nurse Hitchcock. "Your father moved him in there to be quieter."

Ned stayed with Jimmy Bell, who had whistled to him from the gallery; but the other three ran down the long passage connecting the Long Room with the main house, pushed through the baize door, and stepped out into the antlered entrance hall. Mark and Mary knew their way from the long afternoons they had spent with Gervaise and Geraint.

"Oh dear, I'm sure she didn't come walking all through here," panted Mary.

But they need not have worried.

The billiard room had quite clearly been bathed in the sunshine of royalty, and Jim, gaunt and ill in his camp bed, and Hepzie, dumpy in her basket chair beside him, were both bright with the afterglow.

Mary threw her arms around the old woman.

"So she came to you, too," she whispered.

"Yes, she come to me and Jim," said Hepzie proudly.

Jim was looking exhausted but he winked at Mark.

"Wanted to meet you two," he gasped.

"Oh, she didn't!" exclaimed Mark incredulously. "You're just making it up."

"No, he en't, Master Mark, I told her, I did, how Jim cut that great hole in the thatch with me carving knife, and how you two rowed right over the Broad and saved us. And she said she'd like to have talked to you both. Didn't she, Jim?"

Jim nodded.

"That's right, Mother."

"Oh, Hepzie, how wonderful!" cried Mary.

"And she asked after yew and yer Ma, Myrtle," continued Hepzie. "And said we all oughter start buildin' yew a new house right quick, and how maybe she'd find somethin' for yew to put in it."

"Somethin' to put in it?" said Myrtle, flushing a deep red.

"Yes, luv, somethin' out of one of her palaces. She must hev a lot of ole furniture lyin' about in all them houses of hers. Maybe, she could spare a bed or a chair for yer ma."

"Oh, Myrtle," exclaimed Mark excitedly. "I do wonder what she'll send."

"Drove over from Sandringham. That's what she did," said Hepzie in her fat, matter-of-fact Norfolk way. "Bin out all day round her farms, I dare say. And then heard about Reedsmere and drove on to us here."

Suddenly Jim let out a long, painful sigh and rolled his head over to one side, closing his eyes as he did so. He looked unnaturally clean and empty and old. Mary gazed at him conscience-stricken.

"He's very ill," she said softly. "We ought to be leaving him in peace."

"No you don't," smacked out the old woman firmly. "He like to hear you talk. He's just tired and can't be bothered to look. But he like to listen. I know that."

"How do you know?" asked Mark.

"Cos of his hand, of course."

They all looked down at Jim's maimed hand. Mary had never quite come to terms with that hand. It was something she avoided seeing, because she knew the sight would be painful and ugly. It lay now on top of the sheet cupped in Hepzie's right hand, the thumb pressing against her fingers.

"I've bin a sittin' here all day," she explained simply. "Talkin' to him of the old days, and he press me hand when it's a good bit that he like."

Suddenly she began to chuckle deeply in her throat. She, too, was gazing at the maimed hand she was holding.

"She asked which war he'd got that in."

"And what did you say?" gasped Mark.

Jim suddenly opened one eye.

" 'Accident at work, ' Mark boy."

The two Vaughans laughed.

Myrtle looked puzzled.

"I can't think what yer laughin' at," she said. "It must hev been a terrible thing to hev happened."

"So it was, luv," said Hepzie gently. "So it was."

Then they told the old couple of all the things that had happened since Sunday morning when they had left Hepzie at St. Mary's Church after the Candlemas service. Myrtle told them about her mother.

"And she en't dreadfully ill as we thought she were, Mrs. Foulger. The doctors say she'll soon be herself."

Then Mary told them about Mrs. Thrower and her baby in the bottom drawer. And Mark described to Jim the busy scene on the Marram Hills and how the men from the village had worked at the breach half through the night. Then, in a gabble, both the Vaughans told them about the accident to the young soldier.

"Poor boy. Poor boy." Hepzie sighed, drawing air in through her old wrinkled lips. It was a habit of hers that both of them had known all their lives. No grief or bump of childhood had ever been allowed to pass without that consoling, sympathetic whistling of Hepzie's lips.

"Does the doctor think he'll mend?" she asked.

"I don't know," said Mary. "We haven't seen Father since he came back from the hospital. He'd gone out before we woke up."

And then, as was natural, they brought the conversation round to the state in which everyone had found his home. They described the smeared walls, and the drenched furniture, and the floors covered with evil-smelling mud. And then suddenly Mary stopped, her heart torn with pity; for she had seen a tear gather in Hepzie's eye and then slowly trickle down a furrow in her cheek.

"Yew've bin to the cottage, luv?" she asked.

Mary nodded.

"It's in a pretty good mess," burst out Mark. "But Sir Bartlett and Ben Blaza and Dan Ball have shoveled out all the shingle."

"Shingle!" exclaimed Jim and Hepzie together.

"Piles of it. All heaped up against the inside wall. It must've swept in with the sea."

"But Brighton Pavilion's all right," said Mary, trying to make amends. "And we're going to get a tarpaulin to put over the hole in the thatch."

"Very kind," sighed Jim. "All very kind."

One tear was following another fast down Hepzie's cheeks.

"Oh Hepzie, it'll be all right," said Mary. "It really will. We'll all help."

"It's a good village, Mother," murmured Jim, stroking her hand with his thumb.

The old woman gave a great sniff and wiped her eyes with the back of her left hand

"You mustn't mind me, luvs," she said. "Tears come easy-like when yer old."

Then she gave a wry little smile, then a proper grin, and then her deep throaty chuckle.

"Sir Bartlett digging shingle out of me front room," she laughed. "To think I'd live to see a day like that!"

Now that Hepzie seemed happier, Mary began telling her about an argument that she said that they had all had at home.

"You see, Hepzie," she said. "We've got to have all our downstairs rooms redecorated, and we can't agree on what color to choose."

Mark, suddenly understanding what Mary was up to, gave Myrtle a wink.

"Mother wants the drawing room lavender gray, and Father wants it eggshell blue, and I want it ivory white."

"And I want it a brilliant brimstone yellow," burst in Mark.

"What color would you and Jim choose if it were your room?"

Hepzie knitted her brows in thought.

"Shrimp-colored," said Jim suddenly, lying quite still with his eyes closed.

"Shrimp-colored!" exclaimed Mark.

"Yes, boy. The color of boiled shrimps. The prettiest color I've had on me slab for years."

"No, Jim," said Hepzie, shaking her head. "I don't fancy looking at shrimps all me life. All right now and again, you know, but not shrimps for keeps. I'd choose yer mum's lavender gray; that's what I'd choose."

"Here you all are! We've been looking for you everywhere."

Dr. Vaughan was standing in the doorway, smiling at them all.

"Might have guessed you were with Jim and Hepzie, mightn't we?"

Mrs. Vaughan came into the room behind her husband.

"Myrtle, my dear, we want you to come quickly," she said. "You mother has woken up and is asking for you. Canon Crowfoot has got his car working again, and he's waiting to drive you into Norwich."

"How's the soldier, Father?" asked Mary, as they walked out to the car.

"Broken tibia and fibula in both legs."

"Oh, how dreadful!"

"Not nearly as dreadful as I feared. I thought the wheel of the truck had crushed his knee caps. Knee caps are the devil."

"Who did the operation?"

"As luck would have it, Sir Tristram Fanning was in the hospital."

"Will the soldier be able to walk properly again?" asked Mark.

"If Sir Tristram lives up to his reputation," smiled Father, "Corporal Bayly will walk as well as you or I by the summer."

That evening, in their warm, untidy, overcrowded spare room, the Vaughans and Myrtle and the Thrower family sat waiting for the nine o'clock news.

"I wonder if it'll mention the Queen's visit to Reedsmere," said Mark.

"Or the visit of Mr. Macmillan, the Minister of Housing," added his father.

"Why, was he here, too?" asked Mary.

"Yes, this morning, at about half-past ten with quite a big party from Whitehall—inspecting the mending of the breach."

"Ned's nobs," said Mark turning to Myrtle and his sister.

"How wonderfully important Reedsmere has suddenly become," thought Mary.

She knew it was foolish of her to feel so excited. One is not really a nobler, braver person for having passed so close to famous people. Yet she could not help herself.

"I shall never forget today," she whispered to Myrtle. "Today we were part of history."

A minute later Big Ben tolled through the crowded room.

As they sat there motionless, the baby gurgling softly in the drawer, the light of their smiles drained out of their eyes. The terrible tale of the great gale rolled on and on.

A hundred bodies had been recovered from Canvey Island. In the Netherlands, four hundred people were known to have been drowned. In the eastern counties of England, many thousand of families had left their homes. Water supplies were polluted. Warm clothes were needed. Volunteers were called for to mend the sea defenses.

"In a statement to the House of Commons today," said the announcer, "Mr. Churchill said, 'it is not yet possible to measure the magnitude of the loss either in life or material. But it is clear that the catastrophe is one which will require to be treated upon a national basis, and broadly as a national responsibility.'"

As she lay in the bed beside Myrtle's, Mary heard Big Ben tolling and tolling in her heart. A hundred bodies recovered from Canvey Island! In her mind's eye she saw a hundred drowned boys lying under bathing towels on the lawn by the river, just as she had seen the boy from the party of excursionists years ago. Four hundred known to be drowned in Holland! She could not even begin to imagine such horror. "Many families had left their homes." The tears were trickling down the cheeks of thousands of Hepzies from the Humber to the Thames!

Perhaps, after all, it was not an exciting, but a solemn and dreadful thing to be part of history.

New Paint

The early afternoon of the next day, Tuesday, February 3, found Mary sweeping pigeon gray color wash onto one of the walls of the Foulgers' front room. She was pretending that she was conducting the first movement of Beethoven's Fourth Piano Concerto. The bold sweeps of the opening bars were just what was wanted to cover the center of the wall. Behind her, Mark, with his head tied up in a piece of torn sheet and wearing an old school overall belonging to his sister, was sloshing Genoese pink above the door leading into the back scullery. Myrtle, who had whitewashed the ceiling, had scorned to put anything over her head, and now she had just finished washing her hair in a bucket of water and was drying it in front of the fire.

There had never been any doubt in their minds how they were going to decorate the room, for they had agreed at once that the two walls Hepzie looked at as she sat in her own particular chair should be lavender gray, while the two walls that Jim would see as he sat in his chair should be shrimp-colored.

"And we'll paint the doors and window sills white," Mary had said. "And get Mother to tell us what color we ought to dye those poor bedraggled curtains."

Unfortunately the store at Thirlsted had not been able to do better than pigeon gray and Genoese pink; but really they

were not too bad. And as Mark and Mary covered more and more of the walls with the two colors, their interest mounted to enthusiasm.

"Not bad at all," said Myrtle grudgingly, squinting at their work through her dripping hair. "I thought it 'ud look just awful."

When they had entered the cottage soon after an early lunch, they had found the fire out but the atmosphere so hot that they were hardly surprised to find that the walls had dried out. They had lit the fire again but had kept the windows open, for now there was the color wash to dry. The weather had cleared, and the wind was blowing crisp and strong; and Mark and Mary stood in a howling draft on two old fish boxes that they had found in the wash house.

Myrtle looked down at the floor where her hair was dripping water. The boards were bespattered with blobs of gray and pink and white.

"We'll have to scrub that up quick," she said. "Or it'll be awful hard to get off."

"How's the money going?" asked Mary. "Can we afford a pot of floor stain?"

"Ten and sixpence left," replied Mark.

"But that's got to buy the dye for the curtains, too."

"That's enough."

"Ma had some lovely dyes in the shop," said Myrtle sadly. "Such a waste, them all bein' washed away."

Suddenly the flood gates were opened, and Myrtle's and Mrs. Beamish's thoughts about the great gale came pouring out in a rush.

"That's all Ma could talk about yesterday afternoon," she said. "She was glad I'd got the post office stuff, but then she went on and on about the new babies' woolens, and the week's lot of eggs and butter that 'ud only come in on Saturday morning. All them clothes and good food wasted, she said—all floatin' up the Thirl toward Thirlmere. Fat lot it 'ud do anyone 'cept the fishes." Myrtle gave a large sniff.

Mary ran across the room with the paint brush in her hand.

"Oh, Myrtle. I do understand. It's awful for you both. I wish I could do something."

Myrtle gave another large sniff and then smiled.

"You are, Mary. You've just covered the back of me hair with pigeon gray."

"Oh, Myrtle, how awful!" cried Mary.

"You great owl!" roared Mark in delight. "Fancy hugging anyone with a brush full of color wash in your hands!"

By the time they had scrubbed the floor, the light was going fast. The sun was setting in waterish greens and yellows behind Reedsmere Hall, and the corners of the cottage were full of dark shadows.

"We'll have to return tomorrow to do the painting," they decided, and picking up their color-wash pails, the two brushes, the poor, stained curtains, and Hepzie's damp rag rug, they went down to *Donovan*.

As they rowed past the breach, Ben Blaza gave them a great shout and a cheer. They thought for a moment that he was laughing at their strange appearance. Mary's old skiing cap, pulled down hard over her ears, was daubed with white and gray. Mark had splashes of Genoese pink streaked over his face and down Mary's green overall, and Myrtle's hair, which had dried hard in knotty lumps, stuck out like a rag doll's. They realized that they must look an extraordinary sight, floating past in the mutilated *Donovan*. But Ben Blaza was shouting about something far more exciting.

"Look, there's a truck full of empty sandbags," cried Myrtle.

"It's better than that!" yelled Mark. "They've filled the breach. They've filled the breach."

"The village is saved," shouted Mary.

No wonder they were all excited. They all knew that if the gap had not been filled by Thursday's spring tide, the sea would have swept in again. The village would have been under water once more, and all the work they had been doing in the Foulgers' cottage would have been wasted.

They stood up in the sturdy old boat, waving their arms and cheering at the men on the Marram Hills, looking like three clowns from the circus who had just fallen into the whitewash bucket.

When he came in from his rounds in the evening, Dr. Vaughan had news for them all.

"Since the breach is filled, we're going to have a party," he announced gaily.

"A party!"

"Yes. It was Canon Crowfoot's idea. He thought it would do us all good to have a party."

"At a time like this?" said Mrs. Vaughan doubtfully.

"Well, you see, my dear, the whole village has someone they want to thank. And Edward thought that giving a party was the best way of saying it."

"Thank who?" asked Myrtle, looking puzzled.

"I know," burst in Mary. "Rod Cooper."

"Who's he?"

"The American, Myrtle, who saved us all from the church."

"And took me and Jim and Dotty Dick off that horrible roof," added Mark.

"It'll be wonderful to see him again," said Mary quietly.

"What's he like?" asked Myrtle.

Mary smiled thoughtfully. Deep down inside her, the memory of Rod Cooper had lived with her all through the last three days. "A spaceman all covered with rubber," one of the choirboys had shouted. "He's as tall as a tree," another had exclaimed.

Myrtle gave her an impatient nudge.

"Mary, what's he like?" she asked again.

"Oh, just sort of lanky and dark," she said. "You know

what Americans are like; their arms and legs hang sort of loose."

Myrtle nodded. She knew what Mary meant.

"The party's to be on Saturday evening in the Long Room," Father was saying.

"But what about old Mrs. Mobbs and Jim and all those people who are still using the Long Room as their home?" asked Mrs. Vaughan.

"Jim may have to stay where he is in the billiard room," Father replied. "But if he's well enough we had thought of moving him and all the other stretcher cases on to the platform. They'll want to thank Rod Cooper, too. And sitting up in bed watching the young people enjoying themselves will do them all a world of good."

"Who's going to provide the music?" asked Mary.

"Miss Owles has volunteered to play the piano."

Mary made a grimace.

"And Canon Crowfoot has promised to lend a hand."

"That's better," said Mary and Myrtle together. Canon Crowfoot knew all the latest jazz tunes and the newest American musicals.

"Who's going to provide the eats?" asked Mark.

"I expect we shall all do that," said Mrs. Vaughan, warming to the idea of the party.

"And we needn't go back to school until after the week-end?" asked Mary earnestly.

Dr. Vaughan looked her over the top of his glasses.

"Do you really think we'd let you miss the fun, my dear?" he smiled. "We'll pack you both off to school on Monday. That's soon enough."

"And Mary, you must have something new to wear," said Mrs. Vaughan when she came in to kiss the girls good night.

Mary sat up in bed and frowned.

"Don't want anything new," she replied shortly.

"But you must, my dear. Your old dress was really too tight for the Christmas parties, and you seem to have grown inches everywhere since you had measles."

"I said I don't want one, Mother."

Mrs. Vaughan looked at her daughter in astonishment.

"Why not?" she asked. "We'd got it all planned out, Myrtle and I. Hadn't we, Myrtle?"

"Mrs. Vaughan was goin' to drive us into Norwich on Thursday mornin' to buy the lengths of stuff."

"Very simple, you know, Mary. A plain white blouse for you each, with full sleeves, and a gay length of cotton for the skirt. Myrtle wants green, and we thought you'd look lovely in red."

Mary's face broke into a smile, and she threw her arms around her mother's neck.

"I'd love a red skirt," she said. "And may we both have wide black belts? That's what all the girls at school wear for square dances."

"Yes," laughed Mrs. Vaughan. "You can both have huge black belts and pull in your middles as tight as you like."

Mary and Mark and Myrtle spent the whole of February 4 finishing off the decorating of the Foulgers' front room. First they sandpapered the woodwork; then they put on the quick-drying undercoat; and finally, having mixed the high-gloss top coat very thoroughly and having strained it through one of Mrs. Vaughan's laddered nylon stockings, they set to work on the long job of painting the window frames and sills, the baseboard, Hepzie's corner cupboard, and the two doors. They did not do it so well as they had done the walls, because it was a far more difficult task.

Late in the afternoon the room darkened as Ned poked his head through one of the cottage windows.

"Heard 'bout the food for that party?" he shouted.

"No," asked Mark, eagerly. "What about it?"

"Them Yanks from the base hev sent three huge skeps up to the Hall."

"What's inside them?"

"Four cans o' ham—great huge ones—that size," announced Ned, stretching his hands the width of the window. "And cans o' peaches an' pineapples and orange juice."

"Hurray!" shouted Mark, and gave a triumphant slap of white paint on to the windowpane.

"Say, can I come an' help?"

"No, you can't, Ned," said Myrtle severely. "You'll spoil the whole thing."

"Shan't," said Ned indignantly. "No worse 'en what you do."

"Come and stain the floor," suggested Mary. "The light's going, and we want to try and finish tonight. Start over by the fire, Ned."

The Party

There never was such a party in Reedsmere before. Everyone was there. Even Mrs. Beamish. She sat on the platform, propped up in the huge armchair from Sir Bartlett's study, her bandaged head leaning against a fat white pillow and Lady Speke's fur rug tucked comfortably around her knees. And though she looked white and tired, she gazed happily down the length of the room and smiled and smiled. And Jim smiled, as he sat up in bed beside her. And Hepzie smiled. And Mrs. Mobbs sat up in bed with a dreamy, happy, far-off look on her face and nodded her old white head in time to the dance.

Not even Miss Owles's strumming could dampen the fun. And when Sir Bartlett stood up with Myrtle, and Lady Speke chose Dotty Dick, and Dr. Vaughan seized Nurse Hitchcock, and Mrs. Vaughan persuaded old Mr. Clatworthy to take a turn, and the whole village took their places for "Sir Roger de Coverley," the room seemed to hum with joy.

"Oh, what fun it is!" panted Mary to Ned, as they danced together under Canon Crowfoot's and Miss Cotterel's arch.

Every freckle on Ned's face seemed to be smiling back at her.

"Bit of all right," he grinned.

And then they were clapping and clapping as the eldest Peachey girl swung Mr. Clatworthy around between the lines. And then it was Ben Blaza's turn to bow to Mrs. Ball. And down the room they danced again under the arch.

Mark always got very excited at parties. He let out a huge whoop and twirled Sally Blaza round and round so that her skirt flared out like a whizzing top. Then Jimmy Bell whooped too and twirled Jenny Thurgar around. And Ned caught Mary around her wide black belt, and her lovely poppy skirt burst into flower, too. And somehow, Sir Bartlett forgot his party manners and let out the largest whoop of all, and Myrtle's red hair and green skirt flashed round and round in a vivid blur, while everyone clapped for joy.

"There's a truck pulled up outside," yelled Dan Ball over the din. "The driver says he's from Sandringham."

"The Queen's truck," shouted Mark and hurled himself toward the door.

"Myrtle," shouted Mary. "It must be something for you."

Everyone crowded outside and watched excitedly while the driver and his mate unfastened the back of the truck and slowly lifted out two charming mahogany twin beds, an armchair, and a small wooden packing case about two feet square.

"Oh, how wonderful!" exclaimed Myrtle, her eyes dancing. "Fancy Ma and me sleepin' in beds like that!"

"What's inside the box?" asked Mark.

"Let's carry it in to your mother," Canon Crowfoot suggested to Myrtle. "So that she can have the fun of undoing it herself."

So they carried the small wooden packing case up on to the platform and put it beside Mrs. Beamish and waited excitedly while Sir Bartlett went off to find a hammer and chisel and a pair of pliers.

Mrs. Beamish was so moved by the news of the beds and the armchair that she burst into tears, and Myrtle, not having a handkerchief, tried to mop them up with her green skirt.

"Yew don't hev to cry, Ma," she said. "It's a lovely thin' for the Queen to hev done."

"Course it is, me gal," murmured Mrs. Beamish.

She turned her head slightly on the fat pillow.

"It's me head," she confided to Hepzie with the old twinkle back in her eye. "I wanted to laugh, and I bin and gone and made a fool o' myself instead."

Sir Bartlett had returned with his tools, and the village pressed closer around the box.

"Whatever can it be?" wondered Miss Owles.

The last nail was out and the lid was lifted off.

"Something in a lot of packing stuff," Mark informed the outside ring of the crowd.

"Something wooden and carved," shouted Ned.

"It's a cuckoo clock!" exclaimed Mary.

"A cuckoo clock!" they all repeated in astonishment.

"Oh Ma!" gasped Myrtle. "How ever did she know?"

"It's a beautiful clock," said Mrs. Beamish.

Sir Bartlett unhooked the portrait of one of his ancestors and hung up the cuckoo clock in its place. Then he wound it up and put the hands right.

"Oh, Ma, Ma," shouted Myrtle delightedly. "It makes the same awful clackety clack that our own clock made."

They were still waiting for their guest of honor and, since they could not start tea without him and the old people were still panting from the exertion of "Sir Roger de Coverley," Canon Crowfoot sat down at the piano and, looking around at his parishioners, called out, "Come on, all of you. What's it to be?"

" 'Oklahoma!' " cried all the choir and some of the grownups.

" 'South Pacific!' " shouted others.

" 'Oklahoma!' "

" 'South Pacific!' "

But "Oklahoma" won the day.

Canon Crowfoot played the opening bars of "Oh, what a beautiful mornin'," and they all sang the next verse.

And then with a crash came the chorus.

They were intoxicated by the glorious din they were making. Forgotten were the gale and the flood and the mud. Everyone in the village, from Sir Bartlett down to Sandy Catchpole, was floating like summer thistledown over an American countryside, golden with corn.

At the beginning of the third verse a strong young American voice suddenly joined in.

They turned in delight to see their guest standing in the door smiling at them.

How they all roared out the next chorus, as Mark and Ned and Myrtle and Mary and Sandy and Jimmy and all the others swept singing and laughing across the floor toward him!

"Where's yer space suit?" asked Ned.

"How's yer funny little round boat?" shouted Sandy.

"Come along, young man," said Canon Crowfoot, walking across the room with outstretched hand. "You must meet the rest of the village. We oldsters want a chance of making you welcome, too."

And then Rod and the Vicar made the round of the mothers and fathers and grandmothers and grandfathers sitting on the chairs along the edges of the room.

"Eats!" shouted Mark in Ned's direction. "It's time for the eats at last."

And he and Ned and Jimmy and Sandy made a dash toward the door of the canteen.

"Steady on, Mark," called out Mrs. Vaughan. "And before you all make pigs of yourselves, you can bring trays of tea to all the people on the platform."

"What would you like, Hepzie and Jim?" asked Mary.

"Don't know what there is, luv," replied the old woman.

"There's ham and cress stuck between rolls," Mary told them, "and fruit salad and sponge cakes. And Mother's made lots of meringues with real cream in the middle. And there's a batch of Mrs. Lardner's new baked rusks with jam and cream on them. And there's . . ."

"Rusks," said Hepzie decisively. "You go and git Jim and me some o' them rusks."

"And what 'ud yew like, Ma?" asked Myrtle.

"A cup o' strong tea, gal," whispered Mrs. Beamish. "So I'll pull myself together and act proper."

Myrtle squeezed her mother's hand under the fur rug, so that no one else could see.

"Yer doin' fine, Ma," she whispered back. "I'll bring yew one o' Mrs. Vaughan's meringues as well. Mary and me hev eaten three and a half already."

When Mary and Myrtle returned with the rusks and the tea and meringues, they found Mrs. Beamish and Hepzie and Rod and Dr. and Mrs. Vaughan sitting in a circle round Jim's bed.

Rod got to his feet when the two girls entered the circle.

"Why, Mary!" he exclaimed, recognizing her for the first time.

He took her tray from her and looked her up and down.

"My, oh my," he smiled. "How pretty you look!"

Mary blushed crimson with pleasure and embarrassment, while everyone laughed.

"So you see, it was perfectly all right that night, after all," he said. "I found your brother and Mr. Foulger on someone's roof, just like I said I would."

Mary nodded happily, and then suddenly remembered Myrtle.

"This is my friend, Myrtle," she said. "She's living with us till everyone builds her a new home."

And then Mrs. Vaughan told Rod how the post office had been washed away and how Mrs. Beamish and Myrtle and Catty had clung for hours to the top of the coal-house roof.

"And I never saw you, ma'am," said Rod regretfully, turning to Mrs. Beamish.

"We were right back from the street," Myrtle explained. "And we hadn't a flashlight. And each time I shouted, the wind blew me voice back in me mouth."

Suddenly Myrtle turned toward Dr. Vaughan and gave him one of her rare and golden smiles. The whole of her face and hair lit up. Dr. Vaughan smiled quietly back. There was no need to explain. In the warmth and happiness and safety of the Reedsmere party, Myrtle had suddenly recalled the moment when Dr. Vaughan and Mr. Farrow had paddled out of the darkness and had lifted them both off the coal-house roof.

Hepzie was speaking to Rod.

"Bet a handsome young fellow like you hez a girl," she said.

"Yes, ma'am, back home," grinned the young American.

"What's her name, boy?" asked Jim.

"Annie," replied Rod simply.

"Annie," repeated Hepzie thoughtfully. "That's a pretty name."

She seemed lost in the past for a moment, her mind reaching back, through the flood and the wars, to the days of her youth.

"Annie," she said again slowly. Then she looked piercingly at Rod's jet black hair.

"Hev yer Annie got yellow hair the color o' ripe corn?" she asked suddenly.

"Yes, ma'am," replied Rod in surprise.

"And does it curl up wavy-like at the ends?"

"Yes, it sure does," said Rod, still more mystified.

Everyone had stopped talking. They were as astonished and puzzled as the young American.

What was Hepzie getting at? How did she know that Rod's girl had curly yellow hair? Yet, somewhere at the back of her mind, Mary knew she had the answer. Where, quite recently, had she seen straight black hair like Rod's side by side with golden curls?

Suddenly she clapped her hands and burst out laughing.

The locket! Hepzie's mother's blue enamel locket!

In a flash she knew exactly what Hepzie was going to do.

Hepzie put both fumbling old hands to the collar of her dress and lifted the chain off over her head.

"Me mother and I allus wondered who this here locket belonged to," she smiled, her eyes filling with tears. "Now I know, it belongs to you, Rod."

And she handed the locket with its edging of seed pearls to the bewildered young American. Rod read the name *Annie* across the front; and then he turned the locket over and read *Amor vincit omnia*.

"That means Love conquers everything," blurted out Mark.

"And now open it," whispered Mary in Rod's ear. "Put your fingernail into the crack."

And then Rod opened the locket and saw the jet black lock

of hair like his own and the curl of corn-colored hair like Annie's.

"Now, fancy that," he murmured in amazement.

He seemed quite overwhelmed by Hepzie's gift.

"Annie and me'll treasure this always, Mrs. Foulger," he said simply.

When the music started again, Myrtle and Mary linked hands behind their backs, as they had done in the playground over a week ago, and skipped around the edge of the dance floor, waiting for people to claim them as partners.

"Hi, Mary," called out Rod. "Where've you bin all this long time?"

"Come on, Myrtle," said Farmer Smith's eldest son.

And the two couples swung gaily into the Strauss waltz that Canon Crowfoot was playing on the piano. None of them said a word. The girls were carried away with the joy of the dance.

Then after a little time Rod smiled down at Mary.

"Mary," he began shyly, "if Annie and me have a daughter, may we name her Mary—for you?"

Mary flushed in pleasure.

"After me, Rod?" she asked.

"Sure."

"It's lovely of you. But why?"

Rod stammered a little in shyness.

"Cos, cos, you're the first girl I've ever saved," he said.

Mary thought this remark sounded so odd and so charming that her face puckered into laughter.

"And are you going to save lots more?"

"Of course," he laughed.

Then, because the happiness of anyone wanting to name his daughter after her made her feel a little awkward and embarrassed, Mary changed the subject and burst out with her thanks for all that Rod had done.

"You were wonderful, Rod," she said. "You don't know what we feel about the things you did that night. Thank goodness you could swim so well."

"Can't swim a stroke," muttered Rod.

"Can't swim!" exclaimed Mary. "Do you say you can't swim?"

She was so astonished that she stopped stock still in the middle of the dance.

"But how could you have saved us from the church and taken all those people off their roofs in Reedsmere Street?"

Rod shrugged his shoulders and looked sheepish.

"But Rod, the water came right up to your shoulders at Hollow Bridge. It was swirling and eddying all round the place. Rod, you *must* be able to swim."

But the American just shook his head and grinned.

"One false step and you'd have been drowned!"

Mary's eyes grew wide with horror as she remembered Rod with the water up to his neck, gently propelling the rubber boat past Hollow Bridge.

Then she turned toward the platform and over the swell of the *Fledermaus* waltz she shouted:

"Father, Mother! Rod can't swim!"

Going Back to School

This story did not end with the party. Stories seldom do. It did not even end with the cow that Ned had dared Mark to ride, down on the marsh in the middle of morning school. To tell the truth, the cow was one of those thoughtless females who forgot everything the moment that it ceased to happen. As soon as Farmer Smith drove her up to his cowshed early that Sunday morning and gave her a mangerful of sweet, dry hay, the cow forgot all about the howling wind and the salt water licking around her legs all night, and thought only of ruminative, sleepy, cowshed things.

But for the people of Reedsmere the story of the great gale lived on through all their lives. It woke them up. It made them realize that they belonged to one another—that not one of them was alone or set apart. In the horror of that night they had learned that it was their neighbors and themselves, not their houses and furniture and their gardens and fields, that were the true Reedsmere.

As for the boys and girls, they had found something that they thought they had lost.

"It's lovely to see Mary and Myrtle and Ned and Mark together again," Mrs. Vaughan had murmured to Miss Cotterel at the party.

"It's like the old days," the schoolteacher had said. "When I taught them all to read and to count their numbers, and they all tumbled about together in the playground."

The day after the party, Myrtle and the Vaughans left Mrs. Beamish dandling the Throwers' baby by the fire in the spare room and drove to St. Mary's Church.

After the service they took Hepzie down to the top of her lane off the Winterton road. Then they made her sit in the traveling invalid chair that Dr. Vaughan lent to his patients and, between the five of them, they half pushed and half carried it along the sodden ruts toward the sand-strewn garden. Hepzie chuckled away at the bumps and lurches they gave her, and refused to be dismayed by the litter scattered about her home.

"Bless me!" she laughed, when Mark tripped over a broken crate of grapefruit, washed up from some wreck at sea. "Never knew me ole garden 'ud grow fruit like that!"

When they came to the front of the cottage, Mark threw open the door with a flourish.

There lay the Foulgers' front room in all the glory of new white paint and Madonna blue curtains. The gray and pink walls rose in noble defiance of the mud and dreary mess outside. Mary and Myrtle had rowed over earlier that morning and had lit the fire; and now the flames winked gaily in the newly washed ornaments and in the glaze of the green china Brighton Pavilion and danced in the polished glass of Hepzie's father's photograph. The room glowed with warmth.

Hepzie's astonishment delighted them.

"Lord bless us!" she exclaimed. "Who'd a thought me front room would ever hev looked like this?"

"That's the nearest we could get to Jim's shrimps, I'm afraid," Mark explained.

"But if you don't like it," Mary said, looking at the old woman a little anxiously, "you can sit in your chair here, Hepzie and look at the pigeon gray."

"I luv it all, me darlin's," she smiled. "Me and Jim'll allus luv it—and the curtains, too."

"That's Mother," said Mary.

"We can always dye them another color if you think they're too bright," Mother put in.

But Hepzie loved everything. She loved the curtains and the walls and the paint and the dark-stained floor, and even noticed that the old rag rug had been newly washed.

"How a good wash do bring the colors up!" she exclaimed in delight.

Then Father, who had also been to the cottage earlier that day, went to the bottom of the white corner cupboard and brought out three sherry glasses, the rest of the Amontillado, three large tumblers, and a quart flagon of cider.

Ned burst into the room while they were undoing the stopper and pulling out the cork.

"You must drink a health with us, Ned," said Mrs. Vaughan.

"Let us drink to the new Reedsmere," said Dr. Vaughan, raising his glass. "And to the happiness of this room."

Then he looked at Myrtle.

"And let us drink," he said, "to the beautiful new home we're going to build for Mrs. Beamish."

"They've started already," blurted out Ned. "Least, Mr. Blaza and Mr. Ball are walkin' round and round the place where the post office was with a great long rusty chain. And Tom Wright's there, too, scratching his head with a pencil and then writin' things down in a little book."

After lunch they took Hepzie back to Reedsmere Hall to be with Jim, and drove on to the Norfolk and Norwich Hospital to visit Corporal Peter Bayly. Mark and Mary and Myrtle had bought a large box of licorice allsorts from the village shop at Thirlsted, and Kitty Vaughan carried a deep pink azalea in a pot that she had bought in Norwich on Thursday morning.

They found the soldier with his legs stretched up in the air by pulleys. It looked horribly uncomfortable. But Corporal Bayly smiled at them cheerfully as they walked along the ward toward him.

"Did the boys dig that shingle out of the cottage as they promised?" he asked Mary.

"They did it wonderfully," she replied.

"And stuck all Hepzie's china ornaments up in a row on the table," Mark added.

The soldier smiled.

"That stew of yours deserved something very special," he said. "I've never tasted anything like it."

"Nor I," Father laughed.

It was wonderful to see someone who had been so horribly hurt sitting up in bed and looking so merry.

"And will you be in hospital long?" Mary asked him.

"Not if I can help it. I'm due to start training in April."

"Training for what?"

"Half mile. Quarter mile."

"Are you a runner?" gasped Mark.

"Ran for the army last year," he murmured shyly.

"Gosh! How wonderful!"

"Cor!" exclaimed Ned, dislodging a licorice allsort that had got stuck on a back tooth. "Fancy meetin' a runner like that!"

That last night before Mark and Mary went back to school, they had a concert upstairs in the spare room.

"Play a tune on your violin," Myrtle had suggested to Mary. "Yew used to play ever so nice."

"Oh no!" protested Mary. "I haven't practiced for ages."

"That's what you always say when someone asks you to play," grumbled Mark.

"Nothin' posh," continued Myrtle. "Somethin' like yew used to play before yew went off to that school."

" 'Blow the Wind Southerly' and 'The Lass of Richmond Hill?' " asked Mary.

"Yes, and 'Bobby Shafto's Gone to Sea' and that one about the gypsies."

" 'Wraggle Taggle Gypsies O,' " shouted Mark. "Oh, do play that, Mary. It's the only tune I can really sing."

"Well, everyone must promise to join in with Mark," laughed Mary. "The violin sounds pretty awful all by itself. At least it does the way I play it."

Then Dr. and Mrs. Vaughan came up from the kitchen and sang, and Mrs. Thrower, who had gone to bed early to be out of the way, leaned up against the pillows and sang. And Mrs. Beamish and Myrtle and Mark sang. And even Mr. Thrower let out a shy deep rumble when everyone else was making so much noise that no one could possibly hear him. And the baby, though it did not exactly smile, looked as though it was enjoying the din. And Myrtle's Catty sat up by the fire and yawned.

They sang "Green Grow the Rushes O" and "Drink to Me Only" and "I'll Take the High Road and You'll Take the Low," and Mark's "Wraggle Taggle."

Then, just when their throats were getting dry and they felt they could sing no more, Mrs. Vaughan disappeared and returned a moment later with a great jug of lemonade and glasses and a huge plate of hot mince pies.

"Since it's your last night, Mary," said Dr. Vaughan, "I expect you'd like one of your favorite records, wouldn't you?"

"Oh yes," said Mary eagerly. "Are you sure the others wouldn't mind?"

"Of course not."

So they fetched the box of records and the record player, which Mary had carried so carefully into Mark's bedroom on the night of the gale, and plugged it into the bedside plug.

Mary smiled shyly round the room, wondering whether Mr. and Mrs. Thrower and Mrs. Beamish would like her choice, and not knowing what to do.

"I know," said her father. "You needn't say."

And he put on Beethoven's Seventh Symphony.

They all sat in their private worlds, moved and torn and comforted by the great music, till they came to the third movement. At the Peasants' Dance, Myrtle's bare toes started wiggling up and down. Mary caught sight of them in a sudden flicker from a glowing coal.

"Come on, Myrtle," she whispered, smiling.

"Shall we dance as we used to?" she whispered back.

Mary nodded, and the two girls glided from the room. The passage outside was empty, and there was plenty of room for all the arabesques and *pas de chats* one could possibly want.

In the excitement of the *allegro con brio* the girls flew to opposite ends and whirled and swept and flew in an ecstasy of movement and sound. Mary flung both arms above her head and felt as though she were touching the starlit sky that she could see through the uncurtained window. And Myrtle let her red hair stream out behind like wind in an autumn tree.

"It's wonderful, wonderful," they gasped, as they fell in a heap with the final chord.

Next morning they said good-bye to each other, shyly and alone.

"Good-bye gal bor."

"Good-bye gal bor."

"See yew come Easter."

"See yew come Easter."

And then Mark and Mary were sitting opposite each other in the train, dressed in their school uniforms, looking neat, composed, and ordinary. It was odd to be so tidily parceled up again.

And then the rhythm of last night got into the wheels; and suddenly the full orchestra waiting ready inside Mary's head burst triumphantly into Beethoven's paean of victory.

The great gale had come and gone. It had done its worst.

And yet somehow, Mary knew, it was the village of Reedsmere that had won the battle of that disastrous night, not the
wind.

HISTORICAL NOTE

You will find neither Reedsmere Broad nor its village
in a map of Norfolk, for they belong, like Canon
Crowfoot's parishioners, to the pages of fiction. The
great gale of 1953, however, is perfectly true. It
raged across Scotland and the north and east of
England from the afternoon of January 31 till the
following morning. It coincided with an unusually
high tide and caused widespread damage and flood-
ing all along the east coast. Tens of thousands of
people were rendered homeless; hundreds were
drowned. In Holland the disaster was even more
tragic.

I have based the incident of Rod Cooper saving
the choir from St. Mary's Church on the courageous
example of Airman Reis Leming of the United States
Air Force, who on the night of January 31 rescued
twenty-eight people from the roofs of their bungalows
at Hunstanton. For this act of courage he was
awarded the George Medal. Like Rod Cooper he
used an inflated rubber dinghy and, like my hero,
he could not swim.

THE AUTHOR

HESTER BURTON is a well-known English writer of historical fiction for young people. *Castors Away!* was a Carnegie Medal runner-up in England in 1962. *Time of Trial* won the Carnegie Medal in 1963 and was an Honor Book, 1964 Children's Spring Book Festival, New York *Herald Tribune*. Her most recently published book was *No Beat of Drum*. A teacher and editor as well as a writer, Mrs. Burton received an honors degree from St. Ann's College, Oxford University. She and her husband have three daughters and presently live in Oxford, where her husband teaches Greek and Latin.

THE ILLUSTRATOR

ROBIN JACQUES has illustrated many books both here and abroad. He enjoys travel and with his wife and son has lived in France, Mexico, South Africa, and England. He is a Fellow of the British Society of Industrial Artists.